SONS OF SUSANNA

GLEN WILLIAMSON

Tyndale House Publishers, Inc.
Wheaton, Illinois

Williamson, Glen.
    Sons of Susanna / Glen Williamson.
        p.   cm.
    ISBN 0-8423-6073-5
    1. Wesley, John, 1703-1791—Fiction. 2. Wesley, Charles,
1707-1788—Fiction. 3. Methodist Church (Great Britain)—
History—18th century—Fiction. I. Title.
PS3573.I45627S6   1991
813'.54—dc20   91-19411

Front cover illustration copyright © 1991 by Rick Johnson

98 97 96 95 94 93 92 91
8   7   6   5   4   3   2   1

DEDICATION

To Richard L. Aanas,
my brother by reason of marriage and by virtue of the new birth,
this story of the brothers Wesley is affectionately dedicated.

CONTENTS

ACKNOWLEDGMENTS

To Dr. Keith Bell, counselor and educational psychologist, with whom I spent many interesting sessions studying personalities, eccentricities, strengths, and weaknesses of characters involved in the Wesley story, I owe a great debt of gratitude. Editor and teacher Pauline Todd deleted scores of excess commas and slashed my too-long sentences asunder, saving me hours of tedious editing. And my wife, Corinne, whose patience I covet, assisted in years of research, then yielded first place to my computer for months before carefully proofreading the final script. What would an author do without a host of professional friends?

FOREWORD

What more can be written about the Wesleys? I asked myself this question when I received the *Sons of Susanna* from Glen Williamson. After all, I thought, John and Charles Wesley have been bisected by biographers, surveyed by historians, and critiqued by theologians to the point of saturation. Still, I could not forget my discovery of Glen Williamson's gift for writing historical fiction in his book on the Wesleys' mother entitled *Susanna*. Out of loyalty to the author and curiosity about the subject, I started reading.

From the opening sentences the character building begins. John and Charles Wesley become fully human—endowed with gifts that make them great while plagued by quirks that kept them humble. Perhaps in no other book on the Wesleys is the meaning of grace more evident. Much has been written about the saving grace that both John and Charles experienced, by faith, after years of disciplined search for salvation. Glen Williamson tells us the rest of the story with equal drama and special sensitivity. On the long road that John and Charles Wesley traveled, for more than fifty years after their conversion, they encountered public violence, personal alienation, theological conflict, deathly illness, and ministry failure. Williamson faithfully chronicles these events as well as the Wesleys' public acclaim, fraternal love, abounding energy, and manifold success. It is grace that strikes the balance—a grace that is maturing as well as amazing. By the time you come to the moment when John and Charles Wesley put their tested faith into poetry, you will want to weep and sing at the same time. In other words, as a man of grace himself, Glen Williamson has communicated the spirit that makes John and Charles Wesley so powerful in their ministry and so permanent in our memory.

When I finished the book, I asked another question: How can I encourage every person who calls himself a Wesleyan or a Methodist to read this book? It's better than fiction and truer to our history than so many prominent texts that amass the facts but miss the spirit that motivated and matured the sons of Susanna. When all is said and done, it is still that spirit of grace that sets apart the people called Methodists.

David L. McKenna
President
Asbury Theological Seminary
Wilmore, Kentucky

INTRODUCTION

Ten of Susanna Wesley's nineteen children survived infancy. Three of the ten were boys. The Wesleys were poor, but these "sons of Susanna" each managed to graduate from Oxford University. Sammy, the eldest, entered the field of education. He did well in his chosen profession. John and Charles were ordained priests in the Church of England. Their evangelistic zeal, which made them unpopular in High Church circles, was used of God to bring about one of the great revivals of the church.

Herein the story of their lives is cast in fictional format against a backdrop of history as brutal and bleak as mind can imagine.

Sons of Susanna, like its predecessor, *Susanna,* evolved from years of searching for truth regarding the eighteenth-century awakening that saved Great Britain from one of the bloodiest revolutions in history. In an effort to clarify and convey this truth, details—even an occasional personality—have been added to supplement strictly documented material. Lines in conversations are based, when possible, upon the speakers' written records. Successes, failures, strengths, and weaknesses of persons involved have been carefully, prayerfully explored. Halos and horns have been removed from the heads of these sons of Susanna who were as human as you and I. More important, every line is kept in character with personalities, times, and available facts.

Glasgow •

Edinburgh •

SCOTLAND

Newcastle •

Epworth •

Gainsborough •

←To Dublin—
70 miles

ENGLAND

WALES

•Walsall

Garth •

• Oxford

London
•

Cardiff •

•Bristol
• Bath

Salisbury
•

Deal•

• Tiverton

Cowes •

Plymouth •

CHAPTER I
In Wisdom and Stature

Susanna Wesley sat at her desk weeping, which was hardly in character for the lady of the Epworth rectory. But this one time she allowed her tears to flow. Her eldest child, Samuel, Jr., was hurriedly packing his few belongings. At age fourteen, he was leaving for London, two hundred long, hard miles to the south. Except for brief, infrequent visits, he would probably never reside beneath the parental roof again.

Sammy, as the boy was called to distinguish him from his father, Samuel, Sr., was a handsome, strong, mature young man. Although his temper flared upon occasion, he seldom caused his parents a moment of concern. He had completed grammar school and more at the feet of his adoring mother. At the same time, he had received an introduction to Latin, Greek, and Hebrew from his father, whose scholarship was the envy of his peers.

Sammy was leaving for Westminster School with Oxford and eventual ordination in view. It seemed inevitable that this serious, sensitive lad would enter the priesthood of the established church.

His departure from home so early, however, had not been a part of his parents' plan. Even in rural Lincolnshire, the area of Britain wherein the town of Epworth is located, tutors were available to assist earnest students in preparing for entrance to the university. This had seemed the better way to the Wesleys, but no suitable, sober pedagogue could be found to fill the bill for Sammy.

After careful consideration, the parents agreed to send their firstborn off to the wicked city. The Wesleys, always in debt, had no means to support such munificence on their boy's behalf, but an optimistic Samuel found it easy to muster faith in the miraculous. After all, hadn't he one day trudged his way to Oxford with only forty-five shillings in his pocket? Hadn't he graduated four years later, debt free? Couldn't Providence provide for Sammy as well? Susanna reluctantly agreed with the plan.

In the lonely days that followed, the weary mother had little time to dwell upon her sorrow. She still had five children who vied for her attention plus the dreary business of making ends meet on her husband's inadequate salary.

Sammy arrived at Westminster School on a dull, rainy afternoon in September 1704. The ride from Epworth—mostly by horseback, partly by coach—had been rough and tiring. He lifted the latch, opened the door, and stepped into a long, empty hallway with a high, vaulted ceiling. The walls were lined with portraits of serious-looking gentlemen—former administrators, ushers (instructors), and successful graduates, no doubt—who had left their mark upon the school. Tall doors, leading into rooms on either side of the hall, were closed. Sammy had never felt so all alone in all his life. He longed for the rectory and the soft, commanding voice of his meticulous mother. He recalled his father saying, "You'll be homesick, Son, but the Lord will see you through."

His reverie ended with the clang of a bell in some remote area of the building. The doors along the hallway burst open, and young men appeared from every direction. Sammy was suddenly surrounded by a barrage of humanity. Two of the older fellows introduced themselves, welcomed him to Westminster, and escorted him to the headmaster's office.

"Westminster is a good school," they assured him. "You'll like it here. We'll show you around this evening."

"Thank you," Sammy responded. "You're very kind. I'll be anxious to get acquainted."

Sammy received token assistance with expenses from relatives and friends, but for the most part he made his own way. When debts became a burden, he took time off from his classes to work—often for meager pay. This may have been the reason it took him seven years to prepare for Oxford, even though his grades were always at the highest level.

Spiritually, Sammy was never more nor less than lukewarm. The legalistic system his mother embraced as the only gateway to heaven was much too stern for his practical mind to accept. However, he lived a carefully disciplined life because he thought it made sense to do so. He believed also that his emotionally vibrant father, who contended that an inward witness was the strongest proof of Christianity, was equally in error. But he kept these sentiments to himself. He didn't want to hurt his parents; he loved them as they were.

When Susanna's lengthy letters came, exhorting him to keep all the ordinances of God, he answered honestly that he loved the church and took communion regularly. A letter from his father was much more earthy, advising that when a temptation too hard to handle harassed him, he should pen the details of the problem promptly to his pater and drop it in the post. Then he annexed a postscript suggesting that he write such personal missives in Latin, lest his mother should intercept them and be shocked by any indelicacies they might contain.

Sammy smiled as he read and answered with a note of sincere appreciation, saying, "Surely the Lord will not allow me to be tempted beyond that I am able to bear. . . ."

The real Samuel Wesley, Jr., was emerging.

Susanna never ceased to mourn for Sammy, but her fear of the city's evil influence upon him disappeared completely. At age seventeen, Sammy received the high honor of becoming a Queen's Scholar, which relieved him of most of his financial burden at Westminster School. Four years later, he was elected to Christ Church College, Oxford. This last honor occasioned a holiday which brought him back to Epworth. He had been home only once in seven years. An appropriate celebration blossomed with feasting, games, and the sound of music in the old rectory.

Samuel, Sr., was nearly bursting with pride. Susanna, fighting as usual to hide her emotions, maintained a semblance of order in the noisy house. The siblings refused to give their older brother a moment's rest. The girls—Emily, Susanna, Mary, Hetty, Ann, Martha, and Kezzie—some of whom were seeing twenty-one-year-old Sammy for the first time, admired him and loved him. How the older girls must have longed to meet men of like caliber, for the available males of Lincolnshire were coarse and untutored. Sammy appreciated all the flattering attention, but his pride received a blow when he sensed that eight-year-old John showed no special interest in him.

"Jack is friendly, but reserved," Sammy complained to his mother. "I think he doesn't like me."

Sammy inherited his father's fiery temper. The fellows at Westminster School had seen it flare when something displeased him. Now, at a celebration in his honor, his brilliant little brother held a tiny finger on the trigger. Fortunately, he didn't press it. Susanna was blissfully unaware of all this as she and Sammy discussed the boy's future.

"In a couple of years," she said, weighing every word, "John will be ready for special training, but he'll be much too young to make his way as you have done. Whatever shall we do?"

"Perhaps we can get some influential person to nominate him as a worthy student for Charterhouse," Sammy suggested. "Father's salary is certainly small enough to make him eligible. It's a good school, you know. Many important men are numbered among its graduates."

Susanna was acquainted with Charterhouse. A century earlier, an ancient monastery near the old city wall in London, west of Aldersgate, had come into the hands of Thomas Sutton, a man of great wealth. Wishing to devote a portion of his fortune to charity, Sutton had endowed a school and hospital (almshouse) on the site to accommodate eighty male pensioners and educate as many as forty poor but deserving boys at the same time.

"Charterhouse may be the answer," Susanna agreed. "But I don't see how I can allow another of my sons to leave home so early. Your going away was almost more than I could bear, and you were in adolescence. John will still be a little boy."

Sammy smiled. "You wouldn't be a very good mother if you felt otherwise, would you now?" he said, patting her on the shoulder. "Anyway, you'll have time to think it over. Right now, we should go in and join the fun."

As the mother and son entered the noisy room together, four-year-old Charles came running up to Sammy with arms outstretched. The big brother picked him up, for the tiny lad was irresistible.

The celebration ended the following day on a melancholy note as Sammy bade his family farewell and left for Oxford.

John Wesley was born on June 17, 1703. Being the only boy in the parsonage after Sammy's departure, John was the idol of the family. He was as methodical as a clock and sober as a sage, even from the cradle. If lovable baby Charles hadn't arrived when John was barely four years old, he might have been forever spoiled.

The ancient rectory burned to the ground one bitter night in February when John was five. One by one the family escaped the fiery inferno. Then Samuel, counting his children, discovered that John was missing. The distracted father tried in vain to enter the blazing building. Seeing no hope, he dropped to his knees, commending the soul of his son to God. Then a servant caught a glimpse of John through a second-story window and screamed for help. Two men, one standing on the shoulders of the other, retrieved the lad only moments before the roof came crashing in. Samuel's petitions turned to praises. All his possessions went up in smoke, but his family was intact. "I am rich enough!" he shouted.

The following year, a large, red-brick residence was erected. In this substantial, partly furnished home, Susanna set up her school again for the growing children. Obedience without compromise remained the order of the day.

"When a child is corrected," she wrote, "he must be conquered . . . the only strong and rational foundation of a religious education."

Here, as always, she allowed no favoritism to show, but she did allow a special relationship to develop with the obedient, studious John. She wrote, "I do intend to be more particularly careful of the soul of this child than ever I have been that I may instill into his mind the principles of true religion and virtue."

John resembled, imitated, loved, and worshiped his mother. To him, her word was the gospel. He saw in her the acme of perfection. What she believed, he believed. She could do no wrong. When she said, "Son, the only way to heaven is by keeping all the commandments of God," the legalistic tenets she embraced found fertile soil in the open, receptive mind of her little boy. This unusual sense of loyalty became an obsession, a mother-fixation that would follow him all his life. Even so, he couldn't live as well as her unbending rule demanded. Neither, for that matter, could she.

The two years following Sammy's visit passed much too quickly for Susanna. She stretched herself in providing every advantage available for her growing brood. With each child, she set aside an hour per week for private interchange and counsel in which no detail was too trivial, no subject too delicate, no problem too difficult. Then came a foggy day in late November that the weary mother had long been dreading. John, at the age of ten, was being ushered off to London. Charterhouse had accepted his nomination, following a recommendation by the Duke of Buckingham.

His farewell party was marred by tears of sadness, hidden beneath a pretense of joy and laughter. The Wesley girls, with ample reason, found it hard to forgive their parents for sending away a child so young. Six-year-old Charles, who loved, admired, and emulated his brother, was grief-stricken and confused. Life in the Anglican parish-house at Epworth would never be quite the same again.

John entered Charterhouse with shoulders back and head erect. This was good, for being younger, smaller, and smarter than most of the boys, he was subject to ridicule and obscenities by the older fellows. At meal-time, they stole the meat from his place, leaving him only bread and a few vegetables for which he bowed his head and thanked the Lord. Bread and a few vegetables were all he had been used to eating anyway. But he was shocked by the boys' lewd tales and constant bragging of their budding manhood. His sheltered life had not pre-pared him for Charterhouse. He finally succeeded in overriding the problems by ignoring the indecencies and choosing his friends with candor.

But self-condemnation struck a hard blow when his own maturing body carried him into the wonderland of early adolescence. Sexual fantasies tended to convince him that he, like the apostle Paul, was the chief of sinners. The other boys of his age seemed to take it all in stride, but they had not been reared in a village rectory with seven sisters, a "perfect" mother, and a blustering father.

What must God think of me? was often the substance of his musing, for his concept of deity was reflected always in the uncompromising countenance of his beautiful mother. He measured people—especially women—by how closely they approached her standard of perfection. Being unable to analyze his feelings, he needed a friend.

"They say the life of a schoolboy is the happiest in the world," John once stated, "but I am sure I am not happy, for I am not content."

His father's letters were essentially the same as those he had sent to Sammy years before. If the older man had been adept at leading souls into saving grace—an experience he knew but failed miserably to convey—John might have found the Friend he needed.

"Exercise is important," the father wrote. "You should run around the green three times each morning," which, no doubt, was good advice, for John took it seriously. He was fast becoming one of the older boys at Charterhouse, which relieved him of many of his earlier problems. He took advantage of his new status by befriending the younger students. He studied hard. At the feet of the headmaster, Dr. Walker, he excelled in his introduction to Latin, Greek, and Hebrew. From Andrew Tooke, a talented teacher, he pursued the fields of higher mathematics and the sciences, leaving theology to future days at Oxford.

As to his religious life, he at least kept up the forms. Self-examination was always on his weekly agenda. John knew he was a sinner, but a convincing lack of evidence indicates that his transgressions were not fleshly in nature. Even Sammy, who made infrequent visits to the school, seemed pleased with John's progress. In one of his letters home, he wrote, "Jack is a brave boy, learning Hebrew as fast as he can."

Sammy completed his work at Oxford in 1715 and was duly ordained in the Church of England. Susanna and

Samuel received the news with pride and joy. Sammy, however, had little intention of serving the church. His receiving orders was the result of peer and parental pressure and a desire to have a second profession if the need were to arise. He always wanted to be a teacher. Having pursued his education with that in mind, he deemed it a happy day when he was offered the position of head-usher back at Westminster School.

He accepted the job, did well, procured a home, and married an excellent lady whom her friends called Dolly. Following the wedding, he proudly took his bride to Epworth. Susanna and Samuel were elated with their first child-in-law, and the Wesley girls welcomed her to the sisterhood without a dissenting vote. Dolly was pleased with the family, but it was seven-year-old Charles who stole her heart.

"Let us have him," the newlyweds begged. "You'll be sending him away in a few years anyway," Sammy argued. "With us, he will remain right in the family. He will get the best of training, both at Westminster School and the church, and he'll have excellent companions of his own age. And we will see that he gets to be with John again, too."

The parents, stunned by the sudden suggestion, sat with heads bowed in contemplation. But the daughters of the family howled their objections so loudly that Susanna arose and commanded them to hold their peace.

"Your father and I understand your concern," she said. "We have similar feelings too, even deeper ones perhaps than your own. Charles will not be leaving now. We will want him under our care for at least another year. Sammy and Dolly have made an excellent offer that we will take under consideration." She turned to her husband. "You do concur, don't you, Samuel?"

"Yes, of course, dear," he answered sadly. "It breaks my heart to think about it, but we will do whatever seems best for little Charles."

But little Charles had not been consulted in the matter. He sat listening with childish amazement and terribly mixed emotions. His mother rushed to the rescue.

"Forgive us, Son," she cried, putting a loving arm around him. "We were so busy talking about you that we forgot you were in the room. Now you tell us how you feel. Would you like to live in the city with Sammy and his pretty wife someday?"

"I think so," he whispered. Then he ran from the room to hide his tears.

Just one year later, at the tender age of eight, Charles did indeed move into his brother's home.

John Wesley reached the age of seventeen when, despite his youth and smallness of stature, he was ready for Oxford. He left Charterhouse with high honors—elected to Christ Church College with a scholarship that would provide him forty pounds a year. (This was barely enough to underwrite his expenses.) Then, of course, it was his turn to go home for a celebration in his honor.

About noon one Wednesday, Sammy, John, and Charles—the sons of Susanna—drew up their mounts before the imposing, red rectory at Epworth. They arrived amid a flurry of excitement. John was amazed at the changes that had taken place during his absence. His older sisters had matured noticeably; his father seemed much older; and Susanna, still the beautiful mother he adored, was turning gray. But the occasion sparked a spirit of youth and pleasure. Samuel, again, was unable to conceal his pride, while Susanna succeeded, as always, in keeping her feelings securely hidden. Everyone was happy amid a festival of food, games, laughter, music, and dancing. John was wonderfully impressed.

"Today I learned a valuable lesson," he told his mother when they were alone. "I think I have been too somber and serious. I must be more outgoing, friendlier, showing greater interest in others."

"Yes, Son," Susanna concurred. "We are both learning."

At Oxford, John's change in attitude and environment opened a whole new world to him. Socially, he gained confidence in himself and soon became a happy, witty conversationalist. Being generally popular with men, he developed an interest in women, too, but with them he had a problem. When introduced to a lady, he invariably caught himself wondering whether she could arise to the level of his "perfect" mother. His new self-assurance made him even more determined to excel scholastically. He became passionately interested in plays, English literature, the classics, science, and medicine. In discussions, he often became intense, asserting himself with vigorous mind and gesture. When action was inappropriate, he silently held his ground.

A case in point involved an encounter with a certain overbearing professor, Dr. Sacheverell, regarding John's entrance to Oxford. John said, "I found him as tall as a maypole and as proud as an archbishop . . . and I was a very little fellow."

"You are too young to attend the university," bellowed the doctor. "You can know no Greek or Latin! *Go back to school.*"

This barrage of angry pronouncements might have cowered an average fellow. But the dour pedagogue was aiming them at one of the sons of Susanna—one who had inherited a bit of his father's temper as well. John went on to say, "I looked at him as David looked at Goliath and despised him in my heart. I thought, *If I do not know Greek and Latin better than you do, I ought to go back to school indeed.* I left him and neither entreaties nor commands would have brought me back to him." John remained at Oxford in defiance of the haughty professor. The real John Wesley was emerging.

The real Charles Wesley was emerging, too. The lad had difficulty adjusting to his new home in London, sometimes to the despair of Sammy's wife, who tried her best to be a second mother to him. Unlike John, Charles was of stocky build and strong. At school, he was ready to fight for his rights and for those of his friends as well.

One day, Charles caught two bullies giving a little fellow a bad time. The small, Scottish lad was often the butt of practical and sometimes impractical jokes. The ruffians paid no attention to the stocky lad whom they supposed would join them in their fun. Then, the more aggressive bully found himself facing a pair of cold, blue eyes and two clenched fists. Before he realized his danger, he was flat on his back with blood dripping from his nose. Charles turned to the other one, but he was already running away.

"Thank you," the small one stammered. "I'll repay you when I can. I promise."

"Somehow I have a feeling that you will," Charles answered. "I really have."

After a time, Charles settled down to his studies. Sammy, pleased and proud, kept a firm but loving hand upon him. Charles wrote poems—a talent common to the Wesleys. Sammy, a published poet himself, helped him with the fundamentals of the art and encouraged him to continue.

"You write well, Charles," he said. "Practice every day. Sometime you may be noted for your verses."

In Sammy's home, Charles was introduced to such notables as Harley, Earl of Oxford, Joseph Addison, Jonathan Swift, and Matthew Prior. In 1725, at age seventeen, he received the high honor of becoming a Queen's Scholar as Sammy had done years before. Nothing could have pleased the older brother more, a fact clearly documented in a letter he sent to Susanna and Samuel at Epworth:

> Surely you have every right to be proud of your youngest son. Being a Queen's Scholar, he is assured of election to a college at Oxford involving a scholarship to assist him financially. And in the meantime, his expenses here at Westminster will be underwritten, as you know.
>
> I must mention too that he lives well, shunning the sins so common in this environment, and he confesses his love for the church.

Samuel, reading the letter aloud to Susanna, remarked, "If he had also mentioned a love for the Lord, I would be holding a perfect document."

CHAPTER II
The Women of Stanton

At age twenty-one, John Wesley was within a year of receiving a deacon's orders in the Church of England. The year was 1725. Among his more intimate friends was an excellent young man named Robert Kirkham. Kirkham's father was the Anglican rector at Stanton, a day's horseback ride from Oxford. Robert and John, both deeply interested in self-improvement, often studied and prayed together. They were aware that the university was noted for its lack of discipline, with immorality and license running rampant beneath its towers.

"Social life on campus fails to improve, John," his friend told him. "If we want wholesome diversion, we'll have to seek it elsewhere."

"And where is elsewhere?" asked John seriously.

"I would like to take you home with me some weekend," answered Robert. "My sisters invite their friends in to discuss the Word and the classics. They also sing and dance for amusement. Will you go with me?"

John was pleased with the prospect. "Of course," he said. "Your description of home reminds me of the one I remember. I can hardly wait."

Stanton was a quiet village with tree-lined streets hard-packed with gravel and lovely homes and gardens. John's first visit there was everything he could desire. The rectory was old but furnished better than the one he knew at Epworth.

The warmth and love of the closely knit family was like a balm in Gilead to his homesick soul. The rector was a most congenial host. His lady quietly cared for every need of her daughters' friends. After his introduction, John turned his attention to the girls—Sally, Betty, and Demaris—whose interest in their handsome visitor could hardly be concealed. Although John was small, he had fine, well-molded features and wavy, auburn hair that reached his shoulders.

Betty, attempting to curry favor and encourage conversation, smiled at John and said, "Mr. Wesley, your hair is beautiful. You show excellent taste in the way you wear it."

If she thought John would fall for flattery, she was disappointed.

"It's not my taste," he answered, returning her pleasant smile. "It's my circumstances. Wigs and hairdressers are frightfully expensive. A chap I sometimes tutor had his hair piece stolen one evening as he stood at the door of a coffeehouse. But I feel quite secure, for if someone were to grab mine and run away with it, he would be guilty of kidnapping, too, and that's a capital offense, you know."

Everyone laughed. A pleasant mood was established for the evening.

Betty Kirkham—happy, pretty, and outgoing—was a

popular girl. Everyone loved her. Demaris, who was younger and a bit bashful, was cast in the same mold. But Sally, the eldest, was reserved, sober, brilliant, and mostly taken for granted. Not so, however, by their meticulous guest. The evening was hardly half spent before John was fully convinced that Sally was an extremely intelligent, serious young lady, who might indeed develop into another Susanna. He wondered if he were falling in love as he sat with her for a time while the others were playing cards.

"Have you studied Thomas à Kempis?" Sally asked.

"No," said John. "I've read about the little monk and his prolific pen, but I have never taken time to pursue his works. I presume you have?"

"Oh yes," she answered. "I devour them. Excuse me please while I fetch a volume. I will loan it to you if you like."

John watched her as she left the room, admiring her slender build and firm, decisive step. He didn't know that she was engaged to the local schoolmaster. She returned with à Kempis's *Imitation of Christ* and, opening it, pointed to certain underlined portions she believed would interest her new, young friend.

"I'm sorry," she said, following a bit of interesting interchange. "I know you must be awfully busy with the heavy load you carry at the university. Bob says he doesn't know how you do it. Perhaps I shouldn't burden you with this."

"Think nothing of it. I rise at five each morning to improve my mind and refresh my soul," John bragged. "It's wonderful what one can accomplish by adding a couple of hours onto the fresh end of the day."

"Amazing," she whispered. "No wonder you are facing ordination at such an early age. Well, then," she continued. "I will be looking forward to your reaction to the work when you return. You *are* coming back again, aren't you?"

"By all means," he answered. "I haven't enjoyed an evening like this in years."

John returned regularly. Other men were invited, too, but none was as welcome as the little man from Oxford. And ladies came also: a pretty widow, Mrs. Pendarves, whom her friends called Aspasia; the Granville sisters; and the Griffiths, all of whom were interested in serious conversation and the pleasant diversion of socializing with mature, sober-minded young men.

The wholesome effect of these meetings upon John can hardly be exaggerated. He began to take his self-examinations much more seriously. Following his mother's example, he appointed certain hours of each day for private devotions and made long lists of his sins and shortcomings. These included breach of vows, greediness of praise, peevishness, idleness, and sins of thought. He also started rising at four each morning.

As the weeks and months rolled by, his affection for Sally Kirkham took on major proportions. He didn't mention this in letters to his parents, but he reported the deepening of his spiritual resolutions and the resulting changes in his life-style. However, the story of his budding romance, one-sided though it may have been, eventually reached home through correspondence by his younger brother.

At this time, 1726, Charles Wesley was elected to Christ Church College, Oxford. Sammy accompanied him back to Epworth for the traditional celebration. While at home, Charles enjoyed long, intimate talks with his eldest sister, Emily, whom he came to really know for the first time. He found her extremely knowledgeable, possessing the best of common sense.

"We must keep in touch," he told her. They agreed to correspond.

Back at Oxford, John, along with Robert Kirkham, arranged a rousing welcome for Charles, then took him along for a weekend at Stanton. There, the younger Wesley, outgoing and happy by nature, fit into the circle of friends with ease. Over time, Betty couldn't conceal her attraction to him.

Charles, like Sammy, was unhampered by restraints and inhibitions, and he possessed a talent for peering into the problems of others. He hadn't been at Stanton long when he sensed that his brother was treading a dangerous trail with Sally Kirkham. He talked about it with Sally's sisters, discovering that his hunch was valid when he learned of her engagement to the local schoolmaster.

"Does John know about this?" he asked.

"He must have heard of it from someone," ventured Betty. "Sally should have told him, but they are both a bit naive, you know. She may think that his interest is purely platonic, centered in Thomas à Kempis."

"And John may believe that her deepest affections belong to him, that she's waiting for his proposal," suggested Charles.

"Exactly," Betty agreed. "Demaris and I have talked about that, but there is nothing we can say. Sally never discusses her personal feelings with anyone. We are agreed on one thing; we don't want either of them to get hurt."

Charles concurred. He had always looked up to John. Now he felt his duty was to talk with him about his growing friendship with a woman betrothed to another. It was not an easy thing for a younger brother to do.

Only two days before, he and John had had unpleasant words regarding Charles's laxity in spiritual matters. Not that Charles was guilty of any serious transgressions, but he was hardly ready for the disciplined life John was pursuing so religiously. Charles had screamed, "Do you want me to become a saint all at once?" The touchy incident was nearly forgotten—enough so that Charles felt he dared to introduce his deep concern.

"Brother John," he began that evening when they were alone. "I'm worried about you, and I want to help you if I can."

John was perplexed. "What are you talking about?" he asked.

"It's about Sally Kirkham. She is a fine, lovely lady, and I sense that you may be falling in love with her."

"I haven't been trying to keep it a secret, Charles. Why are you concerned?"

"You must remember that you are an ordained deacon in the church, and there are rumors abroad that greater honors may soon be coming your way."

"What of it? I'm not a Catholic. Celibacy is not a requirement in the Church of England—you know that. And if you are concerned about Sally being spoken for, don't you suppose she can terminate her engagement when I make my intentions known? She certainly gives me every reason to believe she cares for me very much."

"Yes, John. Everything you say is true, but love is a strange emotion. Sally may love you as a friend and brother in the church yet never think of you as a suitor for her hand in marriage. Have you confessed your love for her? And if she should accept your proposal, are you prepared to assume the responsibility of a home and family?"

"No, Charles, I'm not. That is the reason I have postponed talking with her about it. I cannot hope to marry for at least six or seven years. Is there anything wrong with a long engagement?"

"I'm sure there is, John, if one of the parties doesn't concur. You may be headed for disappointment. I'm also worried about nasty rumors that might evolve. Today, I will be writing home to Emily. Do you mind if I share my concern with our sister?"

"Go ahead if you wish, little brother. Please don't misunderstand me. I appreciate your interest in my welfare and your boldness in confronting me with it. But I assure you, everything is fine."

John, however, was not so sure of himself the day he received a letter in the post from Emily.

"I am amazed," she wrote, "at how little you know about women. . . . I would not wait one year for the best man in England."

John decided that the time had come to clear the air, to prove to the world—and to himself—that he knew exactly what he was doing. On his next trip to Stanton, he and Sally strolled together beneath the giant shade trees on the rectory lawn as they had done on special, rare occasions before. They discussed the Sermon on the Mount, pinpointing the Beatitudes, marveling at the amazing love of God. It was evening; clouds were gathering in the west. A sunset, not the blazing kind but one soft and peaceful, performed for them. Everything seemed perfect. There John confessed his love to Sally.

Awkward and ill at ease he may have been, but his sincerity nearly broke the maiden's heart. The essence of her love for John remains a mystery. Sally never discussed her personal feelings.

"I must ask you to wait a long, long time," said John. "I can hardly hope to receive a *living* to support us for at least six or seven years. But have no fears, dear lady. I'll be working, saving, planning every step, and counting every hour."

Poor Sally! Poor John! She had to reject his proposal; he had to accept her decision.

They agreed to a casual, friendly relationship and maintained it for many years. Several months later, Sally married the schoolmaster. John danced at her wedding, but no one knew the depths of his remorse. He had felt that he could conquer the world with Sally at his side. Fortunately, even the darkest hour is succeeded by the dawn. John emerged from the lugubrious affair a victor, realizing in retrospect that Sally—wonderful as she may have been—could never become another Susanna.

At Oxford, John Wesley was elected *Fellow of Lincoln* in 1736. This high and unexpected honor improved his position at the university manyfold and made him the pride of the Wesley clan. His father, upon receiving the news, was nearly beside himself with joy. Susanna retired to her room for one ecstatic hour without audience. This was a part of her religion. Even Sammy penned his appreciation in a congratulatory note to his brother with whom he had so little in common. Charles and the girls, of course, were open in their praises. John stated simply that the honor increased his status a lot and his income a little. Actually, in addition to a raise in pay, he was provided a suite of rooms in which to live and to lease when he was not in residence.

Lincoln was a small college at Oxford with a reputation for piety and scholarship. John became lecturer in Greek and presided over the debating society. In his private study, he pursued Arabic, metaphysics, philosophy, and theology. He literally buried his earlier frustrations in his work.

John, with Robert Kirkham and Charles, continued his visits to Stanton, cultivating a friendly relationship with the pretty widow, Mrs. Pendarves. It was much less amorous, however, than the one he had been through with Sally.

His greatest satisfaction during this period came through a marked change in Charles. Each day, the younger brother joined John and Robert in prayers and began to adopt many of the disciplinary measures he formerly had detested. Weeks and months moved along satisfactorily and without incident, until one day John received a disturbing letter from Susanna.

"Can you possibly arrange to come home at least for a season?" she asked. "Your father is ailing and needs an assistant upon whom he can depend. He will have you installed as curate."

The church at Wroote, a small hamlet five miles from Epworth, had been added to the Epworth charge, making the responsibility too heavy for the aging Samuel to bear.

John was in a quandary. How could he say no to his mother? How could he refuse his father? Did one dare ask for a leave of absence so early in his career? John didn't know the answers, but he proceeded to present his case to the proper authorities. Several days later, he was delighted with their decision. It read simply that, since he would be ministering within the pale of the church on a temporary assignment, the request was being granted.

John, with Charles and Robert, spent one last weekend together at Stanton. It was a sad time for all—especially for Charles. He had been leaning more heavily upon his brother than he realized. He was stronger than John in some areas, but in others he was decidedly inferior, and he said so.

"I'm sorry you must go, John," Charles told him. "But I understand. Father and Mother need you more than I do."

John arrived in Epworth to find his father failing in health as Susanna's letter had suggested. He took over a large portion of the preaching load and as much of the administrative detail as possible, which happened to be just the therapy he needed for himself. Calling on the people, dialoging with his father, visiting long and intensely with his mother, writing letters, preparing sermons, and renewing acquaintances with his sisters somehow left him time for meditation, reading, and prayer. Nor did he neglect his Saturday evening periods of self-examination.

John was generally happy with his work, although at times he became tired in body and depressed in spirit. On one such occasion, he was spending a cold, rainy day at his desk, worrying about Charles. He was unable to dismiss the fear that by leaving him, he may have brought about his spiritual downfall. He tried to pray, but no heavenly assurance came. When the post arrived, though, a long-awaited letter from Charles revived his spirit. It began abruptly in a rather muddled fashion, but there was no mistaking its victorious message. It read as follows:

> Verily I think that I shall never quarrel with you again till I do with my religion, and that I may never do that I am not ashamed to desire your prayers. This owing to somebody (my mother most likely) that I have come to think as I do, though I can't tell myself how or when I first awoke out of my lethargy—only that it was not long after you went away.

> Later, John shared the letter with his mother. Few things could have blessed her more, especially the lines referring to herself. She had always felt more than a tinge of guilt for allowing Charles to be taken from the shelter of home so early.

John had been on leave from the university two years when the administration demanded that he return to fulfill his obligation as a Fellow of Lincoln. To leave his father with full responsibility for the churches was not pleasant. John assisted in a reorganization that his father could handle at least awhile. Leaving his mother was another matter. But she was strong.

"Go, my son," she said, "your calling to fulfill."

John went back to Oxford, happy to be reunited with so many old friends. The second weekend following his return, he visited the Kirkhams. His welcome was overwhelming, although he could see that changes were coming. Nothing would be quite the same again with Sally married. But it didn't matter. The women of Stanton had left their mark upon the sons of Susanna.

CHAPTER III

A New Club at Oxford

When John left Oxford to assist his father, Robert Kirkham and Charles realized that their dependence had been upon John more than upon the Lord. It was time for them to launch out on their own. Together, they read Thomas à Kempis from an English translation, the Gospels from the Greek, Psalms and Proverbs from the Hebrew; they wrote verses, sang hymns, and prayed in earnest for grace and direction from heaven. Faithful in attending classes, they kept their grades in the upper level. Ample time was allotted each day for bodily exercise. Charles and Robert could hardly have done better with John by their side.

Other serious students joined them in their seasons of meditation and adopted their carefully disciplined lives. Soon they began to attract attention on campus, becoming the butt of many jokes and slurs. Jokingly, they were dubbed the Holy Club. They didn't mind the nickname, so they adopted it as their official title. They met together, studied, prayed, witnessed, observed communion, and submitted regularly to rigid self-examination. Interest and attendance continued to grow. Then worldly students and some of the professors began to call them methodists.

Eventually, though, owing to increasing persecution and a lack of experienced leadership, interest in the organization began to wane. One ultraconscientious follower, however, remained fanatically loyal—determined to live a completely holy life. His name was William Morgan. William soon became a source of concern to Charles, who feared he might break beneath the physical and mental strain of the stern discipline he imposed upon himself.

At Epworth, John had been made aware of the Holy Club through a letter from Charles. He was deeply impressed. Upon arriving back at Oxford, he was pleased with Charles's spiritual growth, but he saw that the club was gasping for breath. Something had to be done about it.

John—like his mother—was a genius at organization. Following a unanimous vote by the fellows, he became the club's new leader, and it began to grow again. Some of the names added to the roster were: John Clayton, Benjamin Ingham, Thomas Broughton, James Hervey, John Whitelamb, Wesley Hall, John Gambold, and Charles Kinchin.

John established unbelievably stringent ordinances including two full days a week of fasting; never an idle moment; never an idle word; continual inquiry into one another's spiritual state, and more. He demanded that each rule be observed to the letter by every member of the club.

Until this time, the club had been severely introverted—its virtues affecting only its adherents. Then

William Morgan announced that he had been visiting the *castle,* ministering to prisoners on death row.

"What a blessing this ministry has become to me as well as to those poor, wretched derelicts behind the bars," he reported. "I'm convinced that our good works must reach beyond our little cloister if we wish to save our souls."

John Wesley was shaken by Morgan's stinging indictment. "William is right," he said with conviction. "We have been so intent upon working out our own salvation with fear and trembling, that we have forgotten those who fear and tremble just outside our door. We shall become doers of the Word without delay."

New rules were added with further tightening of the old ones. *The care and cure of others* became the watchword. Then, mortification beyond reason began to take its toll, and John became ill. Charles, being strong of body, stood the strain, but his concern for his brother deepened until he decided to share it with Sammy. The eldest of Susanna's sons listened, for he loved Charles, but he was barely sympathetic. He made it plain that he could not condone the fanatical approach to religion that John and Charles were taking. Sammy wrote to Susanna stating his concern, but she could not agree that the perfection her sons were seeking was to blame for John's illness.

"John may be developing a consumption," she answered. "He needs more time for rest."

More leisure, however, was not on the Holy Club's agenda. John slowly regained his strength, but Charles's fears regarding William Morgan were suddenly justified. Through physical neglect, Morgan became emotionally disturbed. The men took turns attending their distracted friend, but within a week he died. Along with sorrow, confusion spread through the ranks of the Holy Club, and nasty rumors swept the campus. Bitter enemies, of course, placed the blame on John. Some even dared to call it murder.

John Wesley was frustrated. Never having suffered such intense persecution before, he unburdened his soul in a letter to his father. Samuel didn't seem to be unduly concerned. For years he had been contending that a great awakening was soon to sweep the Commonwealth. He answered John's disturbing missive, asserting anew that when revival comes, faithful servants of the Lord invariably pay a price. From a Catholic source he quoted, "The blood of martyrs is the seed of the church." He went on to say, "I question whether a mortal can arrive to a greater degree of perfection than steadily to do good, and for that very reason patiently and meekly to suffer evil."

John read those words again. His father had earned a right to write them. Then John read on with growing interest, for Samuel was making personal application of the message.

> For my part, on the present view of your actions and designs, my daily prayers are that God will keep you humble. . . . Be never weary in well doing; never look back, for you know the prize and the crown are before you. Bear no more sail than necessary, but steer steady. The less you value yourself for these unfashionable duties (as there is no such thing as supererogation), the more all good and wise men will honor you if they see your works are all of a piece; or, which is infinitely more, He by whom actions and intentions are weighed will accept, esteem, and reward you.
>
> I hear you have the honor of being styled the

"Father of the Holy Club." If it be so, I am sure I must be the grandfather of it; and I need not say again that I had rather that any of my sons should be so dignified and distinguished than to have the title of His Holiness.

Even Sammy, who agreed with the opposition, penned a note to John in which he said, "I cannot say, I thought you always in the right; but I must now say, rather than you and Charles should give over your whole course, especially what relates to the *castle,* I would choose to follow either of you, nay, both of you, to your graves."

These letters were a tonic to John. He faced the future with renewed zeal and courage, but he had no immediate answer to the problem at hand. A number of students and professors were demanding that the Holy Club be outlawed and banished forever.

Others, though, believed that the fellowship was an instrument of peace devised by God himself. One of their number cried, "Only an awakening greater than Britain has ever known can right the wrongs of this sin-cursed land. Let the Holy Club become an upper room where all with one accord shall pray down the awesome power of Jehovah God! Power to bring an end to human bondage, child labor, drunkenness, prostitution, and starvation."

This group of friendly bystanders agreed that surely the campus of a great university was the place God would choose to initiate such a momentous movement. Even in the face of severe persecution, earnest students continued to join the club, the last of whom was a devout young fellow from Gloucester. His name was George Whitefield.

Word came from Susanna that Samuel was failing fast. John and Charles made their way to Epworth at once and were with their father when he died. All his daughters were there, too. Samuel had called each of his children to his bedside, admonishing them to seek the inward witness of their salvation. His last words to Charles were these: "My son, by all means, be patient. Be steady. The Christian faith will surely revive in this kingdom. You shall see it though I shall not." To John, he said, "The inward witness, Son, the inward witness! That is the proof, the strongest proof of Christianity."

Except for Kezzie, the youngest of the Wesleys, the girls had all left home. Three of them had married. Sammy, who had recently accepted the position of headmaster of Blondells, a school in Tiverton, arrived in time for the funeral. He stayed to assist in settling his father's affairs. Susanna went to live with Emily, who kept a private school in Gainsborough, a bustling market town about twenty-five miles east of Epworth.

John and Charles returned to Oxford to discover that the "upper room" had failed to experience the "Pentecost" for which many friends had prayed. It was dying. Robert Kirkham and others had accepted appointments to churches; some had yielded to discouragement, but a small nucleus was being held intact by George Whitefield. He, John, and Charles met and covenanted to keep the Holy Club alive in their hearts, even though it succumbed completely to the pressures of the world at Oxford.

William Morgan's death was still the talk of the campus. Then, John, too, nearly broke beneath the constant strain of concern and the disciplined life he had chosen. Finally, in desperation, he made a trip to Gainsborough to confer once more with his mother. He remembered the old days. He longed for only that little part of Thursday evening—the precious hour she had spent with him each week when he was a boy. He was that boy again. Her word was the gospel. She could do no wrong.

They met together on a Thursday evening. John planned it that way. Susanna listened to his tale of woe: How he and Charles had both preached with hardly a semblance of success. How he groaned for an assurance of his own salvation. He told her of his love for Sally Kirkham—blaming himself for the way it ended.

"Have I loved women and company more than God?" he wailed. "The thought sometimes disturbs me, especially at the Lord's Table.

"Which reminds me," he continued, "Charles and William Morgan were affected as they ought by the observations you made regarding the Holy Sacrament. I remember your words exactly: 'We cannot allow Christ's human nature to be present in it without allowing either *con* or *trans*substantiation. But that His Divinity is so united to us then, as He never is but to worthy receivers.' Yet, *my* heart did not feel it."

He wept softly as Susanna waited. Then he talked of William Morgan with genuine remorse. "Could it be that I am responsible for his breakdown—his sad, untimely death? God knows I loved him as a brother. He was one of our chief confederates in the struggle to do the whole will of the One who sent us. Or are they right who say it wasn't He who sent us. That I have been demanding a more stringent discipline upon ourselves than God requires?

"As to the claim that we were being 'righteous overmuch,'" he went on almost hysterically, "tell me, Mother, of any instance in our unreserved communications in which you judged us too superstitious or enthusiastic or, on the other hand, too remiss."

"I assure you, Son," she answered, "there was no such instance, ever." She paused briefly, then started to speak again, but John raised a trembling hand to bid her wait.

"Not yet," he pleaded. "I must have evidence of what the Savior holds in store for those who try their best to serve Him. I read it in the Word, but I do not feel it in my heart. You are the one earthly source upon whom I can rely when darkness closes in around me."

Poor Susanna! She had no word of comfort to relieve the turmoil in his breast. Since Samuel's passing, she had struggled with the problem, too. Her husband had truly died in peace. But she, dear lady, after a lifelong effort to please her Maker by every good and perfect work she could employ, did not possess that inward witness that she was a child of God.

"I can only say, Son, that we must do our best and trust His grace for our salvation."

It was not enough, but she had given him the best she had. John felt a note of sadness in her voice.

In one of John's long letters to his mother, he closed with the following words:

> When I observe how fast life flies away and how slow improvement comes, I think one can never be too much afraid of dying before one has learned to live. I mean, even in the course of nature. For were I sure that "the silver cord should not be violently loosed," that "the wheel should not be broken at the cistern," until it was quite worn away by its own motion; yet what a time would this give me

for such a work! A moment to transact the business of eternity. What are forty years in comparison to this? So that were I sure what man has never yet been sure of, how little would it alter the case! How justly might I cry out:

Downward I hasten to my destined place!
There none obtain my aid, none sing thy praise!
Soon shall I lie in death's deep ocean drown'd;
Is mercy there, is sweet forgiveness found?
O save me yet, while on the brink I stand;
Rebuke these storms, and set me safe on land.
O make my longings and thy mercy sure!
Thou art the God of power.

Later, Richard Watson, commenting on the above letter in an early biography of John Wesley, states: "He had, at Oxford, a most painful conviction that he was far below the evangelical standard. He had then, as this letter sufficiently shows, a large measure of 'the spirit of bondage unto fear'; and that after which his perplexed heart panted was the 'Spirit of adoption,' by which he might cry, 'Abba, Father.'"

But back at Oxford, John and Charles continued to preach with little apparent success. Then, from a completely unexpected source, came an opportunity that John believed might be the answer to their problems.

Colonel James Oglethorpe—a heroic, gallant figure—after a successful military career, entered the House of Commons. He was a good and strong man who openly opposed England's notorious debtors' prison system and persuaded Parliament to enact radical reforms regarding it. In 1732 he founded a colony in Georgia—far across the sea—for the principle purpose of providing a place for released prisoners to get a new start. Also, it was to double as a haven for persecuted Protestants.

Preparing to make another trip to the new world with a large group of recently freed debtors, Oglethorpe needed a chaplain to care for their spiritual needs and assist in their management.

He was cognizant of the Holy Club at Oxford and its reputation for piety and discipline, and he was acquainted with the Wesley family. John, he believed, was just the man to handle the chaplain's job. The colonel had been instructed by his board of directors to appoint a man secretary of Indian affairs. He hoped that Charles would accept that position and double also as his personal secretary.

John was delighted when the famous soldier made formal offers of the positions. Charles was less than enthusiastic, but he agreed to go along. "My brother," he said, "who always had the ascendancy over me, persuaded me."

Both John and Charles were interested in foreign missions. This trip, they hoped, would afford them an opportunity to evangelize the American Indians. More important, in saving the Indians, they hoped to find the secret of saving grace for themselves.

When Sammy received the news of his brothers' intentions, he was irate and did his best to stop them. In a letter to Susanna, he presented strong objections to what he called *the whole moronic plan.* "Why in the name of heaven," his pen was fairly screaming, "should duly ordained men who live like angels need to seek salvation anywhere? To cross an ocean to a hostile, virgin wilderness, when good *livings* are available to them right at home is the height of the ridiculous. Only you can stop them," he continued. "John will honor your wishes—you know that—and Charles will follow John without a word."

In the same post, the mother received a letter from John in which he outlined his plans and asked for her advice.

Susanna's profound respect for Sammy's opinion in matters great and small was no secret among the Wesleys. Seldom if ever had she ruled against him. In this matter, pure logic strongly favored his judgment again. But Susanna was slowly undergoing change. That Thursday evening visit with John had had a powerful effect upon her.

"Had I twenty sons," she wrote in answer to both letters, "I would rejoice if they all were so employed."

Sammy sulked. John and Charles prepared to take the Holy Club—in their hearts—to Georgia.

CHAPTER IV

The Good Ship Simmonds

A blazing sunrise streaked through thinning clouds as the morning fog slowly disappeared over London. By noon, October 13, 1735, the first bright, cheerful day in weeks paid England a welcome visit. The *Simmonds,* Colonel Oglethorpe's vessel for the voyage to America, rested in port as peaceful as a swan. Goats, poultry, kine, and swine were fetched aboard. These assured the passengers and crew that fresh meat, milk, and eggs, would enhance an otherwise dreary bill of fare on the two months' journey. Other food supplies consisted of bacon, hardtack, salt beef, smoked herring, butter, vinegar, mustard, lemons, marmalade of carrots, prunes, and sauerkraut. Barrels of water were stored away in the hold.

At Colonel Oglethorpe's suggestion, the Wesley brothers each persuaded a younger man to go along as his assistant. Charles Delamotte, a serious Oxford student and the son of a wealthy London merchant, accompanied John. The two men agreed theologically, but they complemented one another in personality, tastes, and background. Reared in luxury, Delamotte certainly needed the older, wholly dedicated scholar's help down the rugged road ahead.

Charles Wesley chose Benjamin Ingham, the youngest member of the Holy Club, as his assistant. Ingham, a lover of children, dreamed of a day when a pretty companion would present him with little ones of his own. However, he placed this favorite fantasy on hold to accompany his friend to Georgia. The two men made an excellent team.

Ingham and Delamotte shared their problems, divulged their plans, discussed their mentors, studied their Bibles, and prayed together every day.

This sunny day, the four men met in a small coffeehouse to discuss the forthcoming voyage. The ocean loomed dark and dangerous in their imaginations. None of them had ever ventured far out to sea. The thrill of adventure had cast its spell on Ingham and Delamotte. John and Charles were strangely, strongly motivated by a desire to save their own souls.

"There are some rough characters on the passenger list," Ben Ingham reminded his fellows. "Do you anticipate major problems?" He was looking at John.

"Our message will not be popular; we may be sure of that," John answered. "But we must not compromise one jot or tittle. The rules we observed as the Holy Club on campus at Oxford dare be no less viable on the decks of the *Simmonds*. Our success will depend upon that."

"What do you know about the German sect the colonel said would be aboard?" asked Delamotte. "Do you suppose they are strong, devout Christians as he described them?"

"Time will tell," said John. "At least we should be able

to count on their support in dealing with the hoard of godless debtors released from the prisons."

"What about women?" asked Ingham.

"I thought you would be asking that," said Delamotte with a twinkle. "Perhaps brother John can enlighten us."

"Most of the former prisoners are family men with wives and children," answered John. "I understand there will be no single women aboard. Perhaps when we reach Georgia . . ."

This interesting interchange was interrupted by a short, stocky gentleman with a small, black beard, who hurriedly approached the table.

"I am Bishop David Nitschman," he introduced himself to the men in badly broken English. "Twenty-six of my Moravian brethren accompany me to Georgia. One of you will be chaplain aboard, yes?" The man was reciting carefully memorized symbols.

Charles arose and took the proffered hand. "I'm sorry we don't speak German," he said. "But I'll try to make you understand me. My brother John is to be our chaplain."

John stood and gave the man a friendly smile. "I learn new tongues quite easily," he stated. "I am anxious that you teach me German as quickly as possible that I may communicate with you and your people."

"Ya, ve both learn," the bishop answered.

Just then, an overly dressed couple in their early thirties approached the growing party. "I am Dr. Hawkins," the man said, apparently expecting the men to stand and bow. No one did until he introduced his lady. "My wife, Mrs. Hawkins," he snapped.

John tried to be friendly. "I understand that you will be caring for the physical needs of the people aboard. We have something in common. I have been retained by

41

Colonel Oglethorpe to look after the welfare of their souls."

The haughty medic didn't bother to answer, but Mrs. Hawkins gave John a sweet, coquettish smile. John, as always, was amazingly naive. He excused the doctor's brusquerie as a typical trait of the profession. (John's uncle, Dr. Matthew Wesley, was often blunt, too.) The lady's friendly gesture meant to John that she appreciated spiritual values and approved of "men of the cloth." Charles was not so easily fooled. He disliked the doctor and despised his flirtatious wife.

When the group was comfortably seated, a strained relationship was plainly present. Even friendly Charles was unable to initiate a chatty conversation. Then Colonel Oglethorpe appeared with another couple, similar in age and bearing to the doctor and his wife.

"Well, now," said the colonel. "I see my more sophisticated passengers are already getting acquainted. That is good. Let me introduce Mr. and Mrs. Welch, whose interest, they tell me, is in Georgia real estate."

Once again the gentlemen stood in deference to the lady. Charles was as poorly impressed with the Welches as he was with the Hawkinses—especially the women. *There will be trouble aboard the good ship* Simmonds, he mused. *John doesn't detect it. I must have another brotherly talk with him.* Moments later, Charles became certain his judgment was justified. The two women were sitting apart—whispering, giggling, plainly discussing the males of the party, even sometimes pointing to one or another.

Colonel Oglethorpe, sensing that a concealed antagonism was marring the fellowship of the little company, attempted to relieve the strain by making a little speech he had planned to deliver at lunchtime:

"Friends," he began in his best authoritative manner.

"We shall set sail shortly after sunrise tomorrow. Be ready to board ship at four this afternoon. Everything possible will be done to make your journey a pleasant one. We shall have our first meal aboard this evening at seven. We'll follow the shoreline to Cowes and wait there for our convoy. Please pray that today's good weather shall continue. We hope to be out on high seas within several weeks at most. Are there any questions?"

Two rooms in the forecastle were reserved for the Wesley party—the larger one for John and Charles, the other for Ingham and Delamotte. The four were pleasantly surprised. Their quarters, chosen by the colonel to give them as much privacy as possible, were cheerful and comfortably furnished. Even the Hawkinses and the Welches failed to fare as well. The twenty-seven Moravians occupied a small section apart from the other passengers. Colonel Oglethorpe, of course, had his own private quarters.

The meal that first evening was an experience ever to be remembered. Pandemonium reigned! One hundred twenty-four men, women, or children—rich, poor, religious, pagan, refined, coarse, and ordinary—poured into the ship's primitive saloon. Chaplain John Wesley, flanked by his friends, sat with the colonel at the head table. Finally, order was restored.

Mealtimes, thereafter, became important breaks in the heavy schedule of worship services imposed upon the English passengers by John and Charles. (A less stringent discipline was imposed upon the Germans by their bishop.)

Except when dining, the Moravians paid little attention to others on board. But Benjamin Ingham, taking a special interest in children, cultivated an early, close relationship with the introverted Germans.

"Tell me what you have learned about these people, Ben," begged John, when the two were alone one evening. "Do they live up to their reputation?"

"Oh yes," the young man answered. "The Moravians love the Lord and serve Him diligently according to their teaching. However, they fall far short of keeping our Holy Club rules. I learned from the bishop that they were severely persecuted by the papists and, because of their religion, were driven from their country. Count Zinzendorf of Herrnhut graciously received and protected them. He is sending the group to Georgia where free land will be available to them."

"Go on," begged John. "What more can you tell me? I have important, personal reasons for asking."

"I sense that," Ingham replied. "I have listened to them pray and, while I cannot understand much of what they are saying, I am certain that praises far outweigh petitions. Their songs reflect the same sentiment. It seems to me that they are bent upon retaining the faith, practice, and discipline delivered by the apostles."

"You make it sound as though they are actually willing to go the second mile," observed John seriously. "I appreciate your report. Today I begin my study of their tongue. We each have something important to learn from them, I'm sure."

The nice weather turned to wind and rain before the tiny vessel reached Cowes on England's southern shore. There it remained until mid-December. During this period, John preached daily to all who would listen, speaking without notes, which created unusual interest among the worldly passengers. (In the past, he had always read his sermons.) For his own little Holy Club party, he formulated a schedule that was kept religiously. Rising time was four o'clock, followed by a full hour of private devotions. Then, for two hours, the four men read the Bible together, carefully comparing it with the writings of the earliest Christians. Breakfast was at seven, after which they called the passengers together for public prayer. Many, of course, did not respond, but attendance increased daily.

From nine to twelve, John studied German; Delamotte pursued Greek or navigation. Charles, who had recently been ordained priest, wrote sermons to be preached or songs to be sung. Ingham held services for the children. After dinner the four men read to assigned groups of passengers. A public service was held each afternoon at four. Occasionally, at this meeting, children were catechized and instructed before the congregation. At seven, the Moravians held their own worship service, which John attended faithfully. Charles and Delamotte read to people in their cabins. Ingham read to as many as would gather in a meeting between the decks. At eight, just before retiring for the night, the four friends prayed together and discussed the day's successes and failures.

The morning of December 10, the ship moved slowly out of port, headed for America. John and Charles stood on the deck as they passed the needles, watching the breakers explode against the jagged rocks. The great white walls of the island rose to substantial heights. John was reminded of Him "who hath measured the waters in the hollow of his hand"! That evening, the brothers saw a blazing sun go down, buried in the depths of the mighty sea. Charles was poetically inspired. "At dawn tomorrow," he said softly, "there shall be another resurrection from the grave."

The wind was never weary. Full sails carried the *Simmonds* and its human cargo far out on its westward course. Then came a storm! Black clouds, rolling with the wind, moved across the wintry sky. By afternoon of the second day, the elements had taken full control. John wrote in his journal that a great wave swept over the side of the ship, vaulting him to the deck. He escaped serious injury but was so stunned that he scarcely expected to lift his head again until the boundless oceans gave up their dead.

At the mercy of the billows, the little vessel rolled with the turbulent sea. Scores of terrified passengers hovered in mournful silence. They sensed no hope as they watched the lightning's lurid lances and heard crashing thunderbolts. When the black night settled down, the eerie silence turned to wailing cries of utter despair.

"Lost souls on the brink of perdition," whispered John. "And I am one of them."

John and Charles, whose duty it was to encourage and strengthen the people in time of trouble, went to their knees, praying for their own lives. Neither felt worthy of praying for his soul. Their good works in that awful hour, they said, "were as filthy rags." They didn't dare to die. In no way could they hide their fears or speak a word of comfort to those entrusted to their care.

Suddenly, through the turmoil and the gloom, the brothers thought they heard the sound of music! *The angel choir?* The one appearing to a band of lonely shepherds the night that Christ was born? Heavenly hosts coming to the good ship *Simmonds* to welcome the patient pilgrims who were prepared to meet the Bridegroom? Then, happily, John and Charles recognized a psalm of praise and peace and promise. *Of course!* The Moravian brethren were conducting evening vespers at the height of the gale.

About midnight, the winds receded as slowly the storm moved on across the waters. By dawn, streaks of lightning were seen only in the distance. By noon, the sun was trying hard to penetrate the thinning clouds. John, despairing of his spiritual state, sought out one of the humblest of the Moravian brothers.

"We heard your people singing, even when it seemed all hope was gone," he marveled. "Were you not afraid?"

"I thank God, no," he answered.

"Were you convinced that our tiny bark would ride out the raging storm?" John asked.

"No, no," replied the brother. "We thought we were about to meet our blessed Savior."

"But were your women and children not afraid?" John was searching for any spark of light that might illuminate the portentous path he trod.

"No," came the mild reply. "Our women and children are not afraid to die."

In the English service that afternoon, John made an indirect confession of his problem in a powerful discourse:

"I must point out the difference between him that feareth God and him that feareth Him not," he began. "We have just come safely through a devastating storm. I was as frightened as anyone aboard, yet this is the most glorious day I have hitherto seen. I have had a glimpse of a religious experience that keeps the mind at peace and vanishes that feeling which a formal and defective religion may lull to temporary sleep, but cannot eradicate— *the fear of death.*" But the preacher knew that he had only glimpsed—not received—the miraculous experience of which he spoke.

Several weeks later, quiet waters and gentle winds were

blotting out memories of the earlier hectic days at sea. But a storm of a wholly different nature was raging aboard the good ship *Simmonds*. Mrs. Hawkins and Mrs. Welch became enamored of the small but handsome brothers Wesley. While their husbands were occupied with their own interests, the two designing women approached the ministers separately, seeking—so they said—badly needed spiritual counsel. Dr. Hawkins's wife came to John with her distressful tale. Fooled completely, John proceeded to set up appointments with the pretty lady. But when Mrs. Welch tried to interest Charles in her peculiar problems, the neatly packaged plan refused to work.

"If you wish counsel, Mrs. Welch," he said in a practiced, professional tone, "bring your husband with you and we will arrange for times when we can meet together."

That put an end to Charles's particular problem, but he still had to convince John that carnal, ulterior motives attended any confessions he was hearing from Mrs. Hawkins. He finally succeeded, but the end was not yet. Both John and Charles were to learn that *"hell hath no fury like that of a woman scorned."*

Then dawned a day never to be forgotten. Trees, green and beautiful, were seen against a clear blue sky on the ocean's western shore. February 5, 1736, anchor was cast in the Savannah River. The good ship *Simmonds* had reached its destination.

CHAPTER V

New World Fiasco I

John and Charles Wesley stood on the deck of the *Simmonds,* eagerly scanning the American coastline as the ship moved into the mouth of the Savannah River. The pine forest on either side appeared green and warm and peaceful, unlike the cold, white cliffs they gazed upon as they left their homeland.

Just then, a sandy-haired seaman, whom they knew only as Paddy, approached the preachers. He was whistling a merry tune. His clear blue eyes were smiling. "Well, men," he spoke good-naturedly. "We got you safely across the ol' briny, didn't we now?"

"Yes, you did," Charles answered. "Tell me how you knew where to find the port when we were out in midocean. It seems incredible."

"Aye, but it's simple enough for an auld sailor. I could explain it, but it might bore you to the death. To put it in lubber language—no offense intended—we zigzagged our way in a southwesterly fashion from a wet and wintry December in England to a bright and balmy February in Georgia. We've done it before, and I 'spect we'll do it again."

"Do you like it here?" asked John.

"I like to come here," the seaman answered. "But Cork is my home. One day, when I give up the sea, I'll settle there. Me auld mother is still living. She and I will sit and watch the ships come into harbor as we did when I was a wee lad. You can't blame me for dreamin', can you now?"

Just then, Colonel Oglethorpe came hurrying along the deck. The sailor bade the men good-bye.

"Get your party together," the colonel ordered. "We will disembark. You see that green knoll?" The soldier was pointing toward Tybee Island. "The five of us and the bishop will be kneeling there soon to thank the Lord for the safe landing. That's the least we can do."

The brothers heartily agreed. As the colonel went on his way, John was studying the pines. "Look, Charles," he exclaimed. "What an agreeable prospect. The bloom of spring in the depth of winter." He paused, then continued reverently, "A great door and effectual is opened. *Oh,* let no one shut it!"

While the men were engaged in prayer and thanksgiving, the rest of the passengers were disembarking. A warm, friendly breeze from off the shore welcomed the old-world visitors. As soon as the little bank of worshipers arose from the cool, wet grass, the colonel called all the people together where he could address them.

"Bishop Nitschman," he began. "I'm aware that your people cannot understand me. I am anxious that they receive my message as well as the others. I shall speak slowly so you can translate for their benefit." (The bishop and John Wesley had made amazing progress learning one another's language during the many weeks aboard ship.)

"Georgia is the latest English colony to be established on American soil," the colonel explained. "In a political sense, it is vitally important to the Crown. It provides a bulwark protecting Carolina on the north from invasion by the Spanish. For two hundred years, the Spanish have occupied the Florida peninsula to the south of us. Parliament granted a charter and 10,000 pounds for the enterprise. Less than three years ago, I founded Georgia's first settlement, Savannah, which lies not many miles from here. It isn't large—about forty houses—but it continues to grow."

Oglethorpe sensed a spirit of unrest developing among the Germans. He paused, and the bishop signaled a request to speak. "Are we in danger of war?" he asked. "My people want to know."

"War is always imminent," the colonel answered. "My strategy is to avoid confrontation. To be ill prepared is to lose everything. To be well prepared is the best way to avoid conflict. Of necessity, I must prepare our male citizenry at once to defend us in case of an invasion. Only then can we feel secure.

"As you know, my interest in the colony is to provide a safe, ideal refuge for persecuted Protestants and for prisoners released from the debtors' jails. Fortunately, Parliament favors the plan."

Then Oglethorpe revealed his plan, "Bishop, you and your people will go to Savannah. That is where a band of Moravians settled last year. I'm sure they are expecting you.

"John and Mr. Delamotte will go to Savannah, too, where my first order will be for the people to provide materials for a church. Most of you will go to Savannah also. Mr. Wesley will appoint a man to assist you in formulating your plans for your church.

"About sixty people live in palmetto huts 100 miles south of us near the Florida border. I am to organize the settlement at once and make my headquarters there on an island. It shall be called Fort Frederica. Charles," he said, speaking directly to his secretary, "you and Ingham will go with me and remain there. Dr. Hawkins plans to practice medicine in that area. The Welches intend to settle at Frederica as well.

"Are there any questions? If not, you will all board ship again for the night. A boat will be taking me to Savannah at once. I'll return tomorrow."

Services aboard the *Simmonds* that evening were conducted as usual with John attending the Moravian meeting. The bishop preached a simple salvation message —too simple apparently for the methodical, high churchman to embrace. It was freighted with power, however, for John hardly slept a wink that night as his conscience continued to plague him.

The relaxed, rhythmic breathing of Charles became fiercely distracting. *Why is my brother not as disturbed in soul as I am?* John mused morosely. *Perhaps it's because he didn't hear the bishop's message just before we went to bed.*

Before dawn, the daily routine began as usual, but after breakfast, everyone left the ship to explore the new surroundings. Then, about an hour before noon, Colonel Oglethorpe arrived from Savannah accompanied by a Moravian pastor whom he introduced as August Gottlieb Spangenberg. The tall, handsome cleric made a favorable impression on both the Wesleys. His well-molded features, high forehead, grayish-brown hair, and quiet, Christlike spirit fairly oozed strong, intellectual, spiritual grace. John lost no time arranging an interview with the pastor.

When the two men were alone, John came directly to the point. "For years, I have lived the most stringent, disciplined life of which I am capable," he explained. "I serve the Lord with all diligence, constantly seeking holiness of heart. God forbid that I should boast, but I want you to understand my problem. All my efforts are in vain. I lack assurance; I fear death, and my carefully prepared discourses are powerless to save the lost. I have seen God at work among your people aboard ship, but in trying to imitate them, I fail. Tell me, how I can find an answer to my problem? And how should I proceed to convert the natives and minister effectively to the English settlers at Savannah?"

If John expected the pastor to question him regarding his background, scholarship, training, and experience as a minister of Christ, he must have been disappointed.

The good man said simply, "My brother, I must ask you several questions. First, does the Spirit of God bear witness with your spirit that you are a child of the King?" He paused for response that was not readily forthcoming. "Do you *know* Jesus Christ?" he asked, looking straight into the eyes of the little preacher.

"I know He is the Savior of the world," John answered weakly.

"True," replied the Moravian. "But do you know He saves *you?*"

"I hope, sir, that He died to save me."

"I have one more question, Mr. Wesley. Do you know yourself?"

"I do," John answered, but later admitted that he feared his words were vain.

The two men shook hands. The pastor left abruptly. John related the incident to a Moravian brother that evening.

"I felt sure that Mr. Spangenberg was one man who could help me," John explained. "Why did he walk away?"

"Ah, Mr. Wesley," the good man answered. "A wise witness knows when to leave a seeker alone in the counsel of God."

Several days later, John and Delamotte took up their duties in Savannah. Happily, they accepted an invitation to abide in the humble homes of the Moravians until the parsonage became available to them. John needed to observe the Germans practicing their religion in the workaday world. At the close of the first week, he was so deeply impressed that he made an entry in his diary as follows:

> They were always employed, always cheerful, and in good humor with one another. They had put away all anger and strife and wrath and bitterness and clamor and evil speaking. They walked worthy of the vocation wherewith they were called.

John's High Church prejudices were severely rebuked by the apostolic purity of the forms these Moravians followed. He and Delamotte were invited to sit in on a church meeting in which, after a long season of prayer, a bishop was elected and ordained. (Pastor Spangenberg was soon to leave for Pennsylvania; Bishop Nitschman would return to Germany later.) The solemn simplicity of the proceedings made John almost forget the innovations seventeen centuries had projected into church polity. He imagined himself sitting in an early church council with James, the Lord's brother, presiding.

March 7, 1736, John preached his first sermon at Savannah. He officiated at nine in the morning, at twelve, and again at three in the afternoon. He announced that he would administer the sacrament on Sundays and holidays. Prayer meetings each morning and evening were not to be forsaken or taken lightly. The children would be catechized at regular intervals. The schedule was not an easy one for the busy people to abide, but John was so personable and sincere that—up to that point—no word of complaint was voiced by even the hardest of unbelievers.

On the ocean voyage, Delamotte had attended Ingham's services with the children. "I learned a lot," he told John. "I would like to conduct such meetings with the children here if I have your permission. I want to teach them the Bible and more. These little ones need to learn to read and write and cast accounts."

"Of course," John answered. "Make an announcement and get your project underway."

Soon forty children were attending the young man's classes. All went well until some of the poorer children who went barefoot because they had no shoes were ridiculed by those of more affluent families. A morale problem developed that Delamotte was unable to handle. John came to the rescue. Taking over the class for a week while Delamotte tried to work with the Indians, he appeared barefoot before the students every day, without a word of explanation. Soon nearly all the children followed his example. The problem was solved.

For a time, John was more than pleased with the progress he and Delamotte were making. He wrote to his mother, saying, "We are likely to stay here . . . the place is pleasant beyond imagination, and exceeding healthful. . . ." He failed, however, to convey a series of disheartening thoughts that possessed him.

John never ceased to walk in the shadow of his own spiritual problem. It haunted him when he sensed again that his ministry bore no fruit. The hardest blow came when he tried to reach the Indians with the gospel. The red man, he discovered, was not the simple-hearted heathen, hungry for the Word, whom he had visualized when Oglethorpe first asked him to accompany him to Georgia. In defense, he kept himself securely hidden beneath the well-worn blanket of "more holy than thou." He was yet to find that any warmth or satisfaction thus provided would be temporary and degrading.

In an effort to compensate for his failures, John began to impose the strictest—often outmoded—ordinances of the Episcopacy upon the people. Babies had to be baptized by immersion. He denied persons who were not communicants the privilege of acting as sponsors. Anyone having been baptized by any other method had to be baptized again. He even went so far as to refuse Communion to his friend, Bishop Nitschman, because he had not been baptized by an episcopally ordained minister. Even the burial service was denied to any who had died without what Wesley deemed orthodox baptism.

John's popularity was dwindling. One good man faced him with the following rebuke: "I like nothing you do. All your sermons are satires upon particular persons. Besides, we are Protestants; but as for you, we cannot tell what you are. We never heard of such a religion before. We don't know what to make of it."

When John sensed that even Delamotte was no longer in perfect agreement with him, he went to his study despairing. He buried his head in the crook of his elbow as he sat bending over the rough-hewn desk before him. He longed for his mother—the warmth of her spirit, the depth of her love, the strength of her "perfection." He missed Charles. This less inhibited brother had helped him over several hurdles in the past. But John was about to learn that Charles was suffering much greater distress even than himself.

A light rap on the door aroused the near-distracted man from his reverie. Slowly John pulled himself to his feet and made his way to the door. There stood Benjamin Ingham with trouble written across his countenance. Delamotte was by his side.

"Come in, come in," cried John. "I'm glad to see you, Ben. Something tells me, though, that you bring bad news. I hope I can bear it. Already I am the most miserable of men."

The three friends sat together as Ingham prepared to unburden his soul.

"I'm sorry, sir," he began. "I have nothing but grief and pain to share. Charles is in serious trouble. He needs you at once—and badly. He is sick but refuses to see Dr. Hawkins. He is at great odds with Colonel Oglethorpe. I fear for his life. Please go to him before it is too late."

John could see that his young friend was fighting tears. Ingham had traveled three days and nights—partly by foot, mostly by boat—to reach Savannah. His aching body and troubled mind were nearly exhausted.

John was deeply disturbed, but he spoke kindly. "Tell us everything."

"I'll try," said Ingham, taking courage from John's strong voice. "I'll start from the beginning. Please bear with me. This will not be an easy task."

The young man dried his eyes. Then, trying to continue, he yielded completely to his long pent-up emotions. John waited patiently as Delamotte put his arm around his friend.

"It's all right, Ben," he said. "We understand. Take all the time you need."

"Charles was happy when we arrived at Frederica," Ingham began again. "A nicely furnished cabin had been prepared for him, and all seemed well. His problems began, I think, with Colonel Oglethorpe. He was plainly under pressure, and I fear a bit cross as he put Charles to work as his personal secretary. Then the colonel pressed him to get on with his duties as secretary of Indian affairs. Charles seemed to find no challenge in either position, but he tried."

"I'm sure he did," said John.

"Charles, of course, is also the parish priest," continued Ingham. "Being personable and of a happy disposition, he was expected to do well."

"I'm guessing that he failed in all three jobs," said John. "Please get to it. What happened and why?"

"Well," Ingham continued, choosing his words carefully. "Charles never had a chance to succeed. Those two women, Mrs. Hawkins and Mrs. Welch, were bent upon making trouble for him from the outset. It seems they had taken a dislike to Charles aboard ship and were determined to get even with him for something, I know not what."

John nodded. "I know about that," he said. "I'll fill you in later. Please go on."

"The women began telling malicious lies about

Charles to the parishioners before he preached his first sermon. The people believed the stories and refused to accept him. He didn't know why.

"Charles reacted badly, I know. I tried to tell him so, but he wouldn't listen. He saddled the people with a schedule of services and a discipline they were unable to bear. Immersing babies *three times,* for example, which the mothers abhorred. He tried to enforce compulsory attendance, even to the first prayer meeting in the early morning. Four times each day, a drum was sounded to call the people to worship. He made Episcopal ritual and Holy Club rules mandatory. Beneath it all, I fear he was seeking revenge. I say, he reacted badly!"

Ingham paused, realizing the serious indictment he had been making. "Forgive me," he stammered. "I have no right to make judgments. I have expressed an unkind opinion of my superior. Again, sir, please forgive me. I'm sorry."

"Of course," John barely whispered. Ingham's words had condemned him. He, too, had been stumbling blindly down the same unlovely road that Charles had taken. "It's all right, Ben. Right now your reactions are most important to me. There must be more to tell."

"Unfortunately, yes." the young man answered. "Those two miserable women had not finished with their mischief. They approached Charles, asking to confess their sins. I hesitate, sir, to repeat all that was involved, but I have no choice."

"I understand," said John. "Please go on."

"Well, they both confessed to having committed adultery with Colonel Oglethorpe. Whether they meant aboard ship or back in England, I don't know. Anyway, Charles had reason to suspect them of being capable of so sinning. It seems incredible, but he believed their story."

"Oh no," John groaned. "But, *of course,* Charles believed it," he added quickly, coming to his brother's defense. "Women don't generally make up stories like that about themselves."

"Anyway," Ingham hurried on, anxious to finish the unpleasant account. "It became hard for Charles to treat the colonel with any degree of civility. And the colonel, of course, failed to understand the cool treatment he was getting from one who was supposed to be his friend and confidant."

"I can see that Charles was in an awkward position, Ben. Being a priest, he was duty bound to keep the women's secret. What happened next?"

"Ah, that is the sticker," Ingham stated emphatically. "It was the women themselves who let the story out and soon it was being gossiped all over the place. Everyone heard it, I think, except the colonel himself. Then the women had the audacity to go directly to Colonel Oglethorpe, blaming Charles for the lie that was going around. 'He was trying to get even with us for resisting his advances aboard ship,' they said."

"And Oglethorpe exploded!" shouted Delamotte, unable to hold his peace any longer.

"Yes, and he's still exploding," Ingham answered. "The ugly affair has not been settled. The colonel issued an order that Charles be moved to a small cabin with a cold, dirt floor. All furniture was removed. Charles is sleeping on the damp earth, and he has developed a bad cold and cough. Unless he gets help, it may turn into pneumonia."

"What you say, Ben, is hard to believe," said John. "If I didn't know you, I would be sure you made it up."

"I've had to piece it all together," Ingham concluded. "I questioned everyone, including the colonel. He is so deeply hurt and angry that I didn't learn much from him. Charles gave me his side of the story. He still thinks Oglethorpe is guilty. He begged me to take this awful news to you. He wants you to come at once. Please go before it is too late."

John left Ingham in charge of the work at Savannah while he and Delamotte set out for Frederica in a pettiauger, a sort of flat-bottomed barge. Troubles followed them all the way. The second evening they anchored near Skidoway Island, where an early spring flood had raised the water level by more than twelve feet. The two men, soaking wet, wrapped themselves from heads to feet in large cloaks to protect them from the sandflies. Then, lying on the quarter deck, they slept until after one o'clock.

Arriving finally at Frederica, they found the situation exactly as Ingham had described it. Charles was running a fever when his friends reached him at the little cabin. John ministered to his physical needs—no one else seemed to care—and Charles still flatly refused to see the doctor.

"Mrs. Hawkins is insane," Charles warned his brother. "She keeps a gun handy always, and the doctor is madly jealous. Don't ever go near them, John, whatever the problem."

John spent the next hour alone in serious meditation. *What would Mother do if she were here?* he mused. Slowly the tragic picture, emerging from the din, came into focus. John set his jaw. Then, after telling Delamotte where he was going, he made deliberate steps to the office of the colonel and rapped loudly on the door.

Oglethorpe faced him belligerently. "If you have

come to talk about that brother of yours," he growled, "you may as well leave. I don't want to hear his name."

The soldier didn't know it, but he was facing the real John Wesley—son of Susanna, son of Samuel, and a rare combination of the two. The same John Wesley who, as a boy entering Oxford University, had stood up to the great Dr. Sacheverell, even as David had faced Goliath.

"You will hear his name and you will see his face." There was no compromise in the preacher's voice of steel, and his countenance spoke as sternly as his tongue. The mighty colonel cowered beneath the power of this unrelenting, compelling personality of which he had been completely unaware. Then Charles appeared, being assisted up the path by Delamotte.

"Inside!" John demanded. "You men are going to hear me out together."

As soon as his audience was seated, John spoke his mind without hint of hesitation:

"Brother Charles, how could you possibly believe the colonel was guilty of such a gross offense with those selfish, scheming women? You were the one who warned me of their worldly, sensual designs when they first approached us on board the ship. You with your keen discernment should have seen through their carnal plans and despicable lies. At least you could have discussed the evil gossip with your superior, man-to-man, before you made so serious a judgment.

"And *you*," he snapped, turning to Oglethorpe. "You have been gaining promotions all your life by knowing men, sensing their potential, reading their character. How under heaven could you imagine that your secretary, your best friend, your *priest,* could invent a cold, condemning lie about you, whatever the provocation?

"You are both wrong—dead wrong—and it's time for

reconciliation. Time for each of you to ask forgiveness of the other and get on with the work you have been called to do.

"But first . . ." John dropped his voice to a husky whisper. "First, I must ask forgiveness, too, for I have been a fool and blind. If I had been in either of your places in this despicable mess, my conduct would have been worse even than your own. I had the good fortune of coming in late and looking on from the sidelines without involvement. I trust that God has taught us all a lesson that will make us better servants in the future."

All heads were bowed. The room became as quiet as an empty shrine. After a long moment, Charles and the colonel turned and looked at one another for the first time. Then, grinning like two embarrassed schoolboys making up after a playground fight, the two friends arose, shook hands, and locked in fond embrace.

CHAPTER VI
New World Fiasco II

Colonel Oglethorpe was deeply moved by the sudden awakening. Being at heart a kind, religious man, he blamed himself for the whole unlovely affair. With hardly a word, he left the Wesleys with a strong handshake and warm embrace.

"You men stay in my quarters tonight," he said. "I must get away by myself. I'll be back tomorrow. John, take care of your brother. He's very ill."

John was better versed than many practitioners in eighteenth-century medicine. "Delamotte," he commanded, "heat some water and find a small tub. A hot foot bath with a bit of turpentine will help break this cold. Then squeeze some lemons. The juice with a spoon of honey in a little hot water will make just the right tonic. I'll prepare a poultice for his chest."

In record time these primitive remedies were administered and Charles was put to bed, packed away in all the blankets the men could muster. John sat by his brother's side for several hours. Then suddenly Charles was soaking in perspiration. The worst was over.

Oglethorpe returned the following afternoon, renewed—every inch a soldier.

"Charles," he ordered, "as soon as you are able to travel, go to Savannah. You and Ingham will carry on the work that John and Delamotte started. In the light of all that's happened, you can't possibly labor effectively here. John, you and Delamotte will remain for the present in Frederica. If you are cautious, you may be able to win your way with these unruly people.

"Charles, I'm sure that you—and John, too—would find your work much more effective and rewarding if you had wives to assist you. My advice is that you marry as soon as congenial companions may be found." Both men nodded, but Delamotte told Ingham later that their signs of agreement lacked enthusiasm.

When Charles recovered, he bade his friends goodbye and left Frederica—happily and forever. At Savannah, he was thrilled to find that Ingham had started a work among the Indians.

"However did you do it?" Charles asked him.

"It wasn't too hard," Ingham answered. "I met the Musgroves again. They were eager to help me."

Charles listened intently. He was anxious to learn more about this strange couple. "Tell me what you know about them."

"Mrs. Musgrove's mother was an Indian who married an English trader," Ingham explained. "He taught his daughter to speak English. When she was sixteen, she married Musgrove, also an Englishman, who fraternized with the Indians. The couple lived at Cowpen, near an Indian village about four miles from Savannah. They became an excellent team of interpreters who often accompanied King Toma-Chache on his visits with the colonists."

Colonel Oglethorpe, on his first return trip to England, had taken Toma-Chache and some of his party to London where, in full Indian regalia, they were proudly presented to His Majesty, George II.

Charles and Ingham had met the friendly chieftain and his "queen" shortly after they reached Georgia. Accompanied by the Musgroves, the Indians had paid Colonel Oglethorpe and his friends a visit. On that occasion, Ingham heard Toma-Chache—speaking through the interpreters—say to John and Charles, "You are welcome. I have a desire to hear the Great Word. When I was in England, I wanted to hear it. Our nation was then willing to listen. Now we have trouble. The French and Spanish cause great confusion and set out people against the Great Word. Their tongues are useless; some say one thing, and some another. But I am glad you have come."

Then the Indian queen presented the ministers with a gift—two jars, one of milk, the other of honey—after which the royal party returned to their village.

"I remember our first meeting with Toma-Chache. Now you have met Toma-Chache again," Charles marveled. "And you say his village is only four miles away. I presume you have been there."

"Oh yes. And you and I are to go there at once."

Charles was elated with this new prospect of an effective work in America. The days that followed were the only happy ones he knew in Georgia as he indulged in fantasies of success. His dreams, however, were not to be fulfilled. Colonel Oglethorpe appeared with an order for Charles to return to England at once as his personal

representative. One of his duties was to deliver important dispatches to his governing board.

"I will follow you on the next ship," the colonel
assured him, "but it is most important that these docu-
ments precede my arrival. You will come back with me
to Georgia. I need you."

"I appreciate your words," Charles answered sin-
cerely. "I'll come back, but only if I can spend all my
time as a missionary to the Indians."

"I wish I could recommend that, Charles, but the Spanish and French are on the verge of a bloody conflict. The
Indians will be involved in whatever fracas develops. If
you return as my assistant, you will be here to take up
your work when the climate is right. Please think it over
well."

When Oglethorpe was gone, Charles and Ingham
discussed the pending danger of war. They were worried
and sad.

"Maybe there will be a treaty, Ben." Charles spoke
with an artificial note of encouragement. "My advice is
that you proceed with your project as though there were
not a cloud on the horizon.

"I'm sorry I have to leave you," he continued. "When
I get to England, I'll try to induce Mr. Whitefield to
come to your assistance. You two should make a great
team."

John and Delamotte were having serious difficulty trying
to pick up the tangled strands at Frederica. The people
refused to attend the meetings or even treat the men with
ordinary respect.

Then John became ill. He understood the malady, but

he knew that only from the doctor could he procure the proper herbs to repel it. And Charles's warning concerning a visit to the Hawkinses was fresh in his mind.

"I have no choice," he told Delamotte. "A trip to the doctor is my only chance of a quick recovery."

"I'll be glad to get your medicine for you," the young man offered.

"No," said John. "I dare not let it be known that I have reason to be afraid. I will go, trusting Providence to protect me."

Mrs. Hawkins was home alone when John approached the house.

Answering his summons, she opened the door enough to recognize the caller, then slammed it shut. John knocked again. This time she faced him with a gun, which she waved menacingly, demanding that he step inside. He dared not disobey. The demented woman was capable of murder; John saw it in her eyes. He entered the room and closed the door at her command. His only hope was in wresting the weapon from her hand. He watched her closely.

Outside, a child shouted a greeting to a friend across the road. The woman glanced nervously toward a window, and John took full advantage of the slight disruption. His agile mind and body went into action. Grabbing her wrist with one hand, he wrenched the gun loose with the other and tossed it to the far corner of the room. The distracted woman grabbed her intended victim by his long wavy hair and screamed her defiance. John began the painful process of trying to extricate himself from her two strong hands while she cried aloud that she was being attacked by a rapist.

Neighbors heard the cries and came running to the

rescue. Dr. Hawkins, returning home, saw the commotion and heard the screams.

In less than a minute, a half dozen men and women were trying in vain to separate the strange antagonists. Then, following one sharp word from the doctor, Mrs. Hawkins released her grip on the minister's auburn curls and fell limply into her husband's arms.

"What are you doing here?" Hawkins demanded, staring with angry eyes at the hapless John.

The doctor was facing the real John Wesley, even as Colonel Oglethorpe had done some days before.

"I need medicine—some herbs and a bit of bark that I can get only from you," John stated firmly. "When I knocked at your door, I was invited in at gunpoint. Fortunately, I wrenched the weapon from your lady's grasp and tossed it away. You can see it lying on the floor."

Hawkins started to speak, but a neighbor stepped forward and faced him squarely.

"What the little priest is saying is true," he said. "Your wife is a menace to our community. See that you do something about it."

"Woman! Go to your room and stay there," the doctor ordered. The distracted lady, staggering slightly, left the scene. She was clearly a victim of rough pioneeer living, foreign to her nature.

Turning to Wesley, he stated simply, "I'll see that you get your remedies later this afternoon."

"Thank you, sir," John answered. Then, speaking to the group, he continued. "I've been ailing a bit, but I'll be all right by Sunday. At two that afternoon, I will be preaching beneath the oak tree. I expect everyone in the settlement to be present."

And they were.

Several weeks later, as Colonel Oglethorpe was preparing to return to London, he gave final orders to John and Delamotte.

"You have done well at Frederica under the circumstances," he began, "but you can see there is little to be accomplished among these people. I want you to go back to Savannah. The settlement needs a priest, and Ingham wants release from Delamotte's school to give more time to work among the Indians."

"We will go at once," John answered.

"Good, I'll meet you there," the colonel continued. "I plan to spend a couple of weeks in Savannah waiting for my ship to sail. Several important matters need my attention."

John didn't know that one of those important matters would involve him in another painful, distressing experience in the New World fiasco.

Oglethorpe was anxious that John find a wife with whom he could settle permanently in Georgia. And subtle were the steps the colonel took in laying the groundwork for such a union. He believed he knew just the right young lady for the little priest. Upon approaching her family with the suggestion, he received a favorable response. The girl, Sophy Hopkey, was already one of John's favorite students among those he was teaching at Savannah.

Miss Sophy possessed all the natural graces. This slender, blue-eyed maiden enjoyed the elegance of a queen while projecting the innocence of a child. At eighteen, she was the unspoken desire of nearly every unattached male on the frontier.

Sophy was the niece of Mr. Causton, the chief magistrate of Savannah. Causton was also the local storekeeper, real estate investor, and general money-maker, as long as he could keep a step ahead of the primitive law he represented. According to the storytellers, he had come to Georgia to avoid an embezzlement charge in London.

Mrs. Causton was as aristocratic as "uncultured" Georgia would endure.

Both she and her husband were anxious to see their pretty niece properly married, transferring the responsibility of her care—body and soul—to someone else. The Caustons were prepared to make a handsome gift—both money and property—to the man she married, provided, of course, he met with their approval. Unfortunately, few of Sophy's ambitious suitors fit the description. Bowing to the persuasive arguments of Oglethorpe, however, John Wesley came to head the Causton's list of viable candidates for their niece's hand.

The colonel and the Caustons were not without a third confederate in their matchmaking schemes. For some time, Miss Sophy herself had been determined to win the heart of John Wesley. And she possessed the tools to turn the trick, if indeed it could be turned. Ironically, John was blissfully unaware of the plotting and planning in his behalf. Anyway, he was seriously considering celibacy as a way of life.

His mother had set before him an example of perfect womanhood, which he failed to find in any other. From Sally Kirkham, he had learned an invaluable lesson through the ancient agony of heartbreak. A pretty widow, Aspasia, had taught him that Cupid's quiver was still wellstocked with arrows. The women aboard the *Simmonds* had shown him the danger of carnal involvement in the most beautiful of human emotions. John was convinced that all further interest in women—for him—would be purely platonic.

But in his musing, John failed to ponder the powerful presence of human nature innate in all the sons of men. The bell was about to sound again, announcing another hard bout for John with this invisible foe.

Many times, Sophy had come to John for counsel and instruction. Never had he dreamed that he was anything more or less than teacher and priest to this studious adolescent. After all, he was fifteen years her senior. Charles, with his strange sixth sense regarding women, had once warned his brother of danger in a close relationship—even though strictly academic—with such a lovely lass. John had laughed, accusing Charles of being in love with the girl himself.

John and Delamotte were met by Ingham and Miss Sophy when they arrived by boat at Savannah. They walked the mile from the little port to town. Ingham and Delamotte, having many things to talk about, moved on ahead, leaving John and Sophy to trudge along together. The road was rough and steep. They had taken only a few steps when Miss Sophy slipped and—so she said— nearly sprained her ankle.

"I'm sorry, Mr. Wesley," she cried. "Please let me take your arm. I know I shouldn't have come to meet you, but I just had to tell you that I want to get started studying French and German as soon as you can arrange it."

John felt the pressure of her fingers making dimples in the muscle of his upper arm when she stumbled again. Acting purely upon impulse, he caught the girl around her slender waist and held her closely until once again she gained her balance.

"I'm so clumsy," she apologized. "I'll have to watch

my steps more closely. Now about my French and German . . ."

John sat at his desk with his head bowed in deep remorse. He was determined to avoid, henceforth forever, even the touch of that lovely hand upon his own. *Why must I be so weak,* he mused, *when I try to be so strong? Miss Sophy would hate me with ample reason if she so much as guessed my feelings as we walked together into town today.*

Ingham stood in the doorway. "I'm sorry to disturb you, sir," he said. "But tomorrow, I go by boat to Cowpen to converse with Mrs. Musgrove about learning the Indian language. I agreed to teach her children to read and make her whatever recompense she might require. I will be spending three or four days a week at Cowpen, if this meets with your approval."

"By all means," John answered. "I want you to teach me as you learn."

"I anticipated that," said Ingham. "Bishop Nitschman is still here and has asked to sit in on the lessons, too."

"Excellent!" cried John. "It is easier to learn a language when more than one is studying it. I would like to accompany you tomorrow. I am anxious to meet King Toma-Chache and the Musgroves again."

"Of course," Ingham answered. "I was about to suggest it. I'm sure you will be deeply impressed with the progress of this work. You will be pleased to know that the Indians have given me a plot of ground in the middle of a little round hill upon which they are already building a schoolhouse. They have named it *Irene.*"

John was spending long, dreary hours at his arduous tasks. His fifteen-hour days began at four o'clock in the morning. Often, sitting at his feet, was Sophy Hopkey, whose intuition told her that playing the part of an innocent schoolgirl was the way to win the heart of John Wesley. *Take all the time you need,* her inner voice kept saying. *Allow the male to make the first aggressive step in matrimony.* Poor John. *His* inner voice played all kinds of tricks, especially during the two short hours he and Sophy spent alone each day. What an act! Both players were perfect in their parts. Both suffered from apparent failure to accomplish their objectives.

Finally John began to weaken. He was not about to confess his infatuation to Sophy, but he had to share his burden with someone who would understand. He wanted to talk with Ingham, but he had sailed for England to recruit badly needed workers to assist him with his Indian mission. His next choice was Delamotte.

"Sir," the young man said in answer to his query. "I have sensed your problem for some time. You must be aware that Miss Sophy is patiently awaiting your proposal."

"Oh no," John gasped. "Surely she has no such thoughts regarding me." Delamotte smiled. John was begging. "Tell me, what shall I do?"

"I hesitate to advise my senior," the young friend was choosing his words with utmost caution. "But I think you should forget her as quickly as you can."

John next approached Bishop Nitschman whose answer was more emphatic. "Ach," he nearly exploded. "That child is much too young for you. She should find a friend her age. And so should you! Our people have suspected this development and discussed it. We advise you to proceed no further in this business."

While his friends' reactions were disappointing from a

purely human point of view, John was pleased with them. He felt certain that his mother would agree with their verdicts. He knew also that Sophy, with all her pleasing attributes, could never measure up to the inimitable Susanna.

If Delamotte hadn't awakened John to the fact that Sophy was waiting for him to break the silence of their secret passions, much trouble might have been avoided. John could have simply dropped the curtain on the melodramatic charade they had been unconsciously enacting.

But under the circumstances, as he understood them, the meticulous John felt duty bound to level with the lass who had so thoroughly captivated him with her quiet charm. The following day, when the two were alone again in study, John calmly redirected their line of thought from verbs and adjectives to a simple philosophy of life.

Following a few well-chosen, introductory remarks, he stated seriously: "Everyone—and that includes you and me, of course—must ultimately face the future with clarity of mind and honesty of heart."

"Yes," she whispered. "Please go on."

Once again, John Wesley failed to recognize the dangerous bridge he was building. "Now in our case," he continued blindly, "it seems that we might have a good life together. However—"

The naive, little preacher failed to finish his carefully constructed sentence. Suddenly he found himself clasped in the arms of the one he was putting aside forever.

"I thought you would never get around to propose to me," she cried with joy. "Dear John!" (She had never dared to call him that before.) "I can hardly wait to tell my aunt and uncle. Please come to our house as early as you can this evening."

A confused, astonished John—in desperation—opened his mouth to speak, but neither sound nor symbol issued forth as the ecstatic girl rattled on with joy unspeakable. Then, hearing footsteps approaching on the gravel, John pushed her unceremoniously away.

Giggling at the thought of being caught with her arms around the little priest, Sophy touched a finger to his lips and ran out the door.

Glancing back, she cried, "I'll see you tonight." Then she collided with Delamotte.

"What's going on?" the young man cried as he fought to keep his balance.

"Go inside, and John will tell you," Sophy shouted as she headed down the road toward home.

"John? Did she say *John?*" he asked himself. Then, entering the room, Delamotte faced his flustered, frustrated friend.

John Wesley was trying to pull himself together. Slowly his vocal chords began to function as he fought to find a phrase to clear the air. "Delamotte," he barely whispered. "Close the door. I've made a mess of everything. Give me half an hour to contemplate my problem. Then come back, and I'll explain it. I shall need your help."

When Delamotte returned, his dearest friend had fully regained his composure. With painstaking detail, the unhappy man related his pathetic story, pausing periodically for possible reaction which was not forthcoming. Delamotte listened carefully to every word.

"What do you propose that I do next?" John asked.

"Whatever you think is best," the young man answered. He knew that John would make his own decision anyway.

"I'm going to Sophy's home tonight as she requested."

"I know," Delamotte answered. "And you will relate the facts exactly as they stand, embarrassing as they are."

At precisely half past seven, John rapped on the polished, hardwood door. He was admitted by Mrs. Causton, who gave him a most friendly but patronizing smile. A table had been carefully set with the finest linen, exquisite china, and a vase of lovely marigolds from the marshes. An inner door opened. Sophy, dazzling in her newest, prettiest dress, entered the primitive parlor with her uncle, smiling her sweetest, warmest welcome.

John returned their greetings with all the courtesy of an English gentleman. Then, coming right to the point of the problem, he minced no words.

"Miss Sophy, Mr. and Mrs. Causton, tonight I bring the most embarrassing news I ever expect to bear. Will you please find chairs and be seated. This will not be easy for any of us. I begin with a sincere apology to Miss Sophy."

Turning to the astonished girl, he said, "I accept all the blame for making an unclear statement this afternoon, which you misinterpreted as a proposal of marriage. I see no purpose in attempting to explain the details of the error, but I must correct the false impression my words conveyed. I have no intention of marrying anyone now and perhaps never. My calling, as it becomes clearer with the passing of time, is still too hazy for me to guess what the future holds. But I seriously doubt that my work will be conducive to the establishing of a normal, happy home.

"Mrs. Causton, I'm sorry for any trouble my blunder may have caused you. I assume you set this lovely table to celebrate what you were led to believe was your niece's betrothal. Forgive me.

"Mr. Causton, your pretty niece deserves the finest husband she can find. One who will fit into your style of life and give her the peace and happiness that is every decent woman's right to cherish.

"I will go now. May God bless."

There was an unmistakable note of finality in the words, the voice, and the regal bearing of the little priest. *This was the real John Wesley.*

Mr. Causton, flushed with anger, arose and started to speak. "You have said enough . . ."

"And so have you!" snapped Sophy, jumping to her feet. "This is my affair. I'll do the talking."

Staring at the startled, unbelieving John, she issued a volley of unrehearsed threats and insults such as he might have expected from Mrs. Hawkins.

"Now you get out, and don't you ever come through that door again."

By then she was screaming, nearly beside herself. Ah, *this was the real Sophy Hopkey.* John took her at her word and hurried home, an altogether depressed, unhappy man.

Months later, John Wesley—tired, ill, depressed—stood in the bow of a bark, watching the cold, white cliffs of Dover take form in the morning mist. He was home after two disappointing years in America. Ironically, without John's knowledge, George Whitefield was aboard an outbound ship headed for Georgia.

When Delamotte heard of George Whitefield's arrival at Savannah, he lost no time caring for his needs. Since

George was curious concerning the Indian work, the two men went to Irene. Once inside the vacant, one-room schoolhouse, they sat together on two rough benches, while Delamotte briefed the newcomer on the whole New World fiasco. He closed with the story of John and Sophy Hopkey.

Whitefield listened carefully. He felt sorry for John, whom he admired greatly. He knew of his disappointing love affairs at Stanton; now he was hearing of another.

"John made a ridiculous blunder, which Miss Sophy mistook for a proposal of marriage," Delamotte explained. Then he related the story in careful detail. When he finished, the humor of the unfortunate incident struck both young men at the same time. First, they smiled. Then they howled with glee.

"We shouldn't laugh," said Delamotte, trying to recover his sober self. "That misunderstanding caused a world of trouble. Sophy was deeply hurt, which is understandable, but the humiliation of the affair was more than she could bear. Her attitude turned from bad to worse. A month later, on the rebound, she married a Mr. Williamson, who isn't worthy of her little finger.

"John succeeded in keeping his own feelings undercover, but as Communion time approached, he had had enough of her impudence. He faced her as soberly as an archbishop, mentioning several shortcomings in her behavior. 'You must make amends,' he told her.

"Sophy left in a huff and related the incident to her aunt. Mrs. Causton expressed regret to John for Sophy's behavior and asked him to present his objections in writing."

"And he did, of course," said Whitefield.

"Yes, but there was no response from Sophy, and she made no move to mend her ways. Then, on Sunday, without having announced her intention, she had the audacity to present herself with other communicants for the sacrament."

Whitefield smiled broadly. "John refused to serve her," he guessed.

"Yes, and you might say that was the beginning of sorrows. With instruction from her uncle, she started litigation, suing for defamation of character. Sophy's friends talked about it so incessantly and vociferously that John felt the whole colony was lined against him."

"Was it?" asked Whitefield.

"Of course not. But after appearing in court no less than a half dozen times with no settlement in sight, John decided to return to England. He made public announcement of his intention, and no attempt was made to restrain him. To avoid possible trouble, though, he sneaked away in the night and went to Charleston. I met him there, then I came back to Savannah.

"Since then, he has been completely vindicated. Mr. Causton was soon caught misappropriating funds. He lost everything: job, reputation, elaborate home—and he may lose his wife. Sophy's marriage is on the brink of disaster, too."

"I'm glad you are here to tell me all this," said Whitefield seriously. "I knew something was terribly amiss when I received a note from John on board ship about the third day out of Deal. One of those small, speedy sailboats caught up with us to exchange mail and deliver a passenger who had missed the sailing. The note, without a word of explanation, almost demanded that I return home and forget about America. I was confused, for I had received a letter from him some weeks earlier in which he begged me to join him in Georgia."

"I understand your frustration," said Delamotte thoughtfully.

"I was severely tempted to return on the speedboat," continued Whitefield. "I would have, I guess, but suddenly a still small voice reminded me of the Old Testament prophet who turned back from his appointed course. Another prophet had told him that such was the will of the Lord."

"I remember that story," said Delamotte. "The man was slain by a lion, wasn't he?"

"Right," said Whitefield. "So I came on to Georgia."

"Well, I'm glad you did," the other responded. "I fear John's depression spilled over on me a bit. I never knew a man to be so utterly dejected. He seemed to have lost his self-esteem along with any hope for the future. It's hard to understand, for everything about him was so out of character with the Wesley you and I both knew so well.

"I'm certain of this, though," Delamotte continued. "The problem, basically, is a spiritual one. The Moravians teach that salvation is a work of grace, wrought instantly through faith in the atoning blood of Christ. Neither John nor Charles could accept that. They contended that so great a blessing must take time for a soul to merit."

"I know," said Whitefield. "I went through all that, too, when John and Charles left me in charge of the Holy Club. I was under such pressure that I became ill, desperately ill, and I was not aware that a remedy, free and complete, was available for the asking. I knew no more that I must be born again than if I had never been born at all.

"Then I read a treatise that Charles had left with me. It asserted simply that true religion is a union of the soul with God. A ray of divine light burst in upon me. I trust I shall have reason to bless God for it through endless ages, for in the seventh week of my trouble, God was pleased to remove the heavy load. He enabled me to lay hold of His dear Son by a living faith. Joy unspeakable and big with glory filled my soul.

"The Moravians are right. It takes but a moment for God through Christ to do that which man cannot accomplish in a lifetime of earnest endeavor."

Delamotte sat with bowed head for several moments. Then, facing his young companion, he stated firmly, "George, you'll never know how much I appreciate your clear testimonial. John and Charles will find their way. So will I. So will Ben Ingham and a million more."

"Our friend Ingham has already laid hold of saving grace," said Whitefield. "He is preaching with success wherever he finds a pulpit open to him. I have no fear for John and Charles. God is preparing them for something greater than we can guess. They will see the light. And when they do, they'll let it shine. I shall be praying for you."

George Whitefield found everything in Georgia exactly as Delamotte described it. In his first letter back to England, he wrote as follows:

> The good which Mr. John Wesley has done in America is inexpressible. His name is very precious among the people; and he has laid a foundation that I hope neither men nor devils will ever be able to shake.

CHAPTER VII
Empty Hands

No wayward son, having served a term in prison, was ever more disposed to avoid the family he disgraced and the friends he failed than was John Wesley. Upon returning home from two long, unsuccessful years in Georgia, his troubled soul was bathed in darkness. He wondered if God had said again to Satan, "All that he hath is in thy power; only upon himself put not forth thine hand." His depression deepened as he walked along Front Street in the seaport city of Deal.

John longed to see his mother. But in his muddled mind, the shame he bore was such that he couldn't bear to face her. He felt sure that his brother Sammy, who had opposed the American venture, calling it a "whole moronic plan," would say, "I told you so." And who would debate him? John was fearful that Delamotte's aristocratic parents would drive him from their door if he honored his friend's request to bring them greetings. His oldest, dearest friend of Stanton days, Robert Kirkham—

now an Anglican priest serving a growing congregation—would surely deny him the courtesy of his pulpit. Even his brother Charles, whose failure in the new world mission was greater than his own, would blame him for the troubles he endured.

John was determined to avoid each of them as long as possible. But Colonel Oglethorpe was one to whom he was duty bound to report at his earliest convenience. Following that, he would be obliged to appear in person before the Georgia Board of Directors to give an up-to-date report of the work. He made plans to meet the colonel the following day.

Before he had walked a city block from where he disembarked, John heard someone shouting his name. He turned to face an old acquaintance from Oxford days—Stinky Stafford—who was forever ridiculing the Holy Club.

"Well, no! If it isn't the wee Wesley," Stinky cried, snickering at his own impertinence. "Still trying to convert the world, I'm told. I must be the lucky one, always running into someone who would like to save my soul. Only a couple of days ago, I was down at the docks where I met your old friend, Whitefield. He was getting ready to board ship. Funny thing is, he said he was going to America to help you convert the natives. Wouldn't he be surprised if he knew I was talking with you only a mite from where he and I were standing?"

"What ship was he boarding?" John asked excitedly. "I must get word to him before he is too far out to sea."

Finally, having gained the information he needed, John hurried back to the harbor. There he scribbled a note to Whitefield in which, among other things, he said, "When I saw that God was carrying you out by the same wind that brought me in, I asked counsel of Him. His answer was, 'Let Whitefield return to London.'"

John confronted an important-appearing officer in uniform. "Sir," he said. "I have a letter to my friend Mr. Whitefield, who is aboard your outgoing vessel. Can you get it to him?"

"But of course," the officer answered with a hint of amusement. "We are preparing to send a small sailboat out immediately bearing one of His Majesty's emissaries who arrived too late for the sailing. 'Overslept,' he said. Ha! His bloodshot eyes explained the reason. Don't worry. We'll see that your man gets the message."

Colonel Oglethorpe, deeply engrossed in his accounts at a friend's home in London, was aroused by a light, hesitant rapping at the door. Being alone in the house, he laid aside his papers to answer the summons. To his surprise, there stood John Wesley.

"John!" he cried. "You are the last person I expected to see. You appear to be ill. Come in. I was just thinking about you. We need to make plans for the future of Georgia."

The colonel's enthusiasm and friendly manner helped in dispelling the deep depression that had long been sapping the strength and confusing the mind of his chaplain.

"I guess you can say that I've been through the fire," said John sadly. "I'm sorry to have failed you. I don't deserve your kind words. Everything went wrong, and I have no one to blame but myself."

"Come now," the colonel remonstrated quickly. "I received word from a friend regarding the troubles you were forced to face in Savannah, which he explained were not your fault. I feel responsible for your difficulty with Miss Hopkey and her uncle."

"I . . . I don't understand," John stammered.

"It was I who first suggested that Causton's pretty niece would make an ideal companion for you. I misjudged the family completely. Anyway, now we can relegate all that to the past. I am anxious that both you and your brother return with me to Georgia. Charles came home about as discouraged as one can get, but he's doing much better now."

"Where is he?" John asked.

"This past week he has been with the Delamottes at their mansion near Bixley, several miles east of London. He will be mighty glad to see you."

"The Delamottes!" John exclaimed. "I didn't suppose they would ever speak to either of us after the way they resented our taking their boy to America."

"I understand that George Whitefield broke through their prejudices," the colonel said. "They heard him preach several times. Now the family is seeking peace of soul. They are looking to Charles for help.

"You must go there, of course, but not tonight. The directors are meeting to consider some requests I have made for arms. I cannot be present, for I have an important engagement at Westminster. You will meet with them and report the progress we are making. Please paint the prettiest picture your conscience will allow. That is the same request I made of Charles. He carried through very well."

"I'll try," John answered. "Tomorrow, I'll go to the Delamottes' and have a chat with Charles."

That evening, John gave his report to the twenty-one-member board of directors. Later he went gratefully to bed for the first good night's rest in months.

The following morning, a cold, February wind swept through London. John stepped into Cannon Street, wrapped his great coat around him, and boarded a coach for Bixley. At the elaborate residence of the Delamottes, a servant answered the summons and announced John's arrival. Moments later, a queenly lady entered the room where a blazing hearth welcomed her guest. Tall, slender, immaculate—Mrs. Delamotte was a most impressive person.

"I'm so happy to see you, Mr. Wesley," she said, motioning to a chair by the fire. "We had no idea you were in London. I'm anxious, of course, to hear the latest of my son. Your brother has been our delightful houseguest for the past week," she rattled on. "He went for his morning walk about an hour ago. He'll be back any moment. He talks about you all the time. I can hardly wait to see his happy smile when he discovers you are here."

John, amazed at the peace the few friendly words brought to his troubled soul, leaned forward, looking straight into the eyes of the one he had feared to face. "I've been such a failure," he admitted honestly. "I'm altogether unworthy of your kindness.

"About your son, I hadn't realized how much he resembles you. He is doing well. Whatever would I have done without him? He is so young and strong, asking nothing but the will of God. I left him at Savannah in charge of the work we started there.

"George Whitefield is on his way to Savannah now. I wrote him a note, suggesting that he abandon his plan to go to Georgia and transfer to an incoming boat. I doubt that he will do it. Your son will be delighted to see him in Savannah. The two are about the same age and have many traits in common. They should make an ideal team."

"Oh, that Mr. Whitefield," the lady answered. "What

a preacher he is! My husband and I attended his services. We haven't been the same since. Now we are studying the Scriptures with your brother. I'm so happy that you have come, for surely you can help us find salvation. We are a bit confused, for Charles seems to be seeking, too."

Steps were heard on the graveled drive that led to the door. Through a window Mrs. Delamotte saw Charles approaching. Without a word, she hurried to open the door.

"Come in, Charles," she cried. "You have company." Then, quietly and discreetly, she withdrew, leaving the brothers alone to enjoy their reunion.

For nearly an hour, the two men discussed their experiences abroad. John spoke in detail of his problem with the Hawkinses. "You told me never to go near the doctor's home. I should have taken your advice."

"The Lord must have had his hand on the whole sordid affair," said Charles. "It was a dangerous thing you did—and a brave one. I shudder to think of what might have happened if I had been in your place."

John related the unhappy story of his infatuation with Sophy Hopkey. "Again, I should have taken your advice, Charles," he said. "You can see I need you."

"We need one another," the brother answered thoughtfully. "I guess we were meant to stick together. This has not been an easy year, John. Many times I have longed to discuss my problems with you. But one good thing has been happening. That Moravian interpretation of saving grace becomes clearer to me every day. Only yesterday, in my meditation, I was reminded of Jesus saying to the Pharisee, 'Thou are not far from the kingdom of God.' I felt he was saying the same to me."

"Jesus must have been doing exactly that," said John. "Tell me more of your experiences since returning home."

"All right, I'll begin from the very first. The day I arrived, John, I was ill and longed to see Mother. I took a coach to Tiverton where she was living with Sammy and his family. I was so depressed and beaten that I didn't care how much our brother might deride me for ignoring his advice regarding our going to America. I was certain that Mother would side with me, even though the story of my failure would disappoint her deeply. To my surprise, my welcome was genuine enough, even from Sammy. He saw that I needed rest and food. Mother was kind, telling me how much I reminded her of Father.

"'Have you been careful in keeping the commandments?' she asked. 'I am sure your venture was not as futile as you imagine it. Your witness will bear its own fruit when time has had opportunity to ripen it for the harvest.'"

Charles paused. "My own faith, John, doesn't reach such proportions."

"Nor does mine," John answered sadly.

"Before I recovered my strength, I went to London," Charles continued. "I knew Oglethorpe was counting on me to deliver some important papers and to give my report to the board of directors. I delivered the papers, but when I arose to speak, my voice was so weak the men couldn't hear me. The chairman read my report.

"The next day I came here, for Delamotte had made me promise to visit his family. I approached the door with fear, but the parents were so anxious to hear from their son, they invited me in and ministered to my needs. Apparently they were blaming you for luring their son to Georgia."

"Had they already become interested in seeking salvation?" John asked.

"No, but several months later, when George Whitefield was preaching to great congregations, they attended his meetings. Then they began seeking the Lord. George was preaching, not with persuasive words of man's wisdom, but with demonstration of the Spirit and power. The churches could not contain the crowds that thronged to hear him.

"I began making rounds, renewing old acquaintances at Oxford, preaching at the *Castle,* returning to see Mother, and visiting our sister Martha and Wesley Hall. They seem to have a good marriage. Hall was duly ordained and appointed to a living at Wooten. I had a good visit with sister Kezzie. Unlike the other girls of our family, she has no interest in men, but she longs to be converted. She said, 'Charles, I want to become a new creature.' I'm ashamed to say that I felt utterly helpless as I prayed over her and recited Pascal's prayer for conversion."

"Kezzie was always an exceptional girl," said John. "If I had stayed in Georgia, my plan was to ask her to come and make a home for me. I was seriously considering the celibate life.

"I know what you mean, Charles, when you say you felt utterly helpless. I feel that way all the time. I sense, though, that you are making progress."

"I still have a horrid fear of death, John. That 'love of God that casteth out fear' is an illusive article. Whitefield claims that he received saving grace the moment his faith 'touched the hem of the garment.' His good works, he said, were of no avail."

"Sounds like the Moravians," John observed thoughtfully.

"Right," cried Charles. "You know, John, our father

died in perfect peace. He had no fear of the unknown. Perhaps we should have taken him more seriously when he talked of an inward witness as the strongest proof of Christianity."

"I have thought of that many times, Charles. I am certain that Mother dwells upon it, too."

"My problem, John, is that I have never been able to accept the teaching that salvation is an instantaneous work. That seems as absurd as saying one need not spend years in college to graduate. Just believe that whatever the books teach is true and receive your diploma."

John smiled. "I agree that instant conversion is hard to abide. I think, though, there is a basic error in your simile. Grace and knowledge may be close relatives, but they are not twins. Peter wrote that one must grow in both areas.

"I preached to a large audience in Deal a few nights ago, just before going to London to meet the colonel. I mentioned my contact with the Moravians in America. Later, I was approached by an intelligent, young man named Peter Bohler. Peter said he was a Moravian, not by birth but by conversion. He contends firmly that he was led into faith by Count Zinzendorf with only a bare knowledge of the Bible. Since then, he has studied theology at the University of Jena in Thuringia, Germany. Apparently he has developed into a successful evangelist and has been ordained by the count for work in Carolina. He stopped in Britain to improve his English."

"I would like to meet him," said Charles.

"You will, I'm sure. He was looking for a place to stay. I directed him to the Huttons in Westminster with a letter of introduction. They'll treat him well. I've stayed with them many times. He may be a great help to us."

Mr. Delamotte—a stout, handsome, intelligent man of commerce—arrived home late that afternoon. He welcomed John heartily. After a bountiful dinner of roast lamb, laced with mint and seasoned with herbs, he gathered his family around the glowing hearth to study the Word of God. He was an open-minded gentleman, ready to face objectively any new thoughts and interpretations of the Scriptures that might be projected.

John sensed that the lady of the house was a bit pragmatic and opinionated, seeking texts to prove her prejudices. *I can't be critical, he mused soberly. I've been making the same mistake all my life.*

During the course of the study, Charles brought up the subject of instantaneous conversion. "Unrealistic," he called it. Then, as he continued to expound his views on the controversial issue, Mrs. Delamotte began nodding her head in agreement. (She hadn't yet learned to shout *Amen,* as many of Whitefield's admirers had been doing in his meetings.) Charles, stimulated by her symbol of approval, became more and more eloquent.

John, sensing that Mr. Delamotte was quietly weighing the matter, feared that Charles's dogmatic utterances might hinder the spirit of the meeting. When opportunity afforded, he made a carefully worded comment, hoping to ease the strain.

"I, too, have had difficulty accepting that doctrine," he stated. "But I must admit there are many Scriptures that endorse it. Consider Paul on the Damascus road."

The reaction was exactly opposite of that he had intended. His pronouncement brought everyone to attention. Sensing that he was facing some severe opposition, John decided that a bit of personal testimony might act as ointment on the bruise.

"I went to America to convert the Indians," he said, "but, oh, who shall convert me? I have a fair summer religion while no danger is present. But let death look me in the face, and my spirit is troubled, nor can I say, 'to die is gain.'"

Mrs. Delamotte, flushed with anger, arose and left the room. Charles was aggravated, too—stunned by his brother's open defiance of his stated opinion. His good sense, however, warned him that an ounce of diplomacy might be worth a ton of debate. He remained in the room for awhile, then left abruptly, closing the door behind him a bit too noisily. John got the message, but he took it in stride.

The following morning, everyone was congenial again, enjoying a hearty breakfast together.

John, by then, was ready and eager to visit his mother. Susanna was staying temporarily at Salisbury, a town southwest of Oxford, on the way to Tiverton.

"Let us find Peter Bohler and take him to Oxford," John suggested to Charles. (The Delamottes begged them to stay, but both men thought it wise to depart and return again later.)

"We will introduce Peter to our friends," John explained. "I would like to preach again at the *Castle*, then go to Salisbury to spend several days with Mother before going on to Tiverton to pay my respects to Sammy."

Charles concurred.

John, Charles, and Peter Bohler traveled by coach to Oxford. Scholastically, the twenty-five-year-old German was on a level with Charles—several steps below John—but far in advance of both brothers in spiritual discernment. They discussed theology, with John standing foursquare on his legalistic views.

"I have always considered my mother to be the greatest, strongest Christian I ever expect to meet," he stated firmly. "More than once, I heard her say, 'Son, the only way to heaven is by keeping all the ordinances of God.' That is the way I try to live. That is what I have preached for years."

"My brother, my brother," the Moravian exclaimed. "That philosophy of yours must be purged away!"

"I know now that it is not enough to save me," John answered, apparently taking no offense from Peter's sharp rebuke. "Charles and I went to America not only to save the Indians but to save ourselves. We failed on both accounts."

"John and I have discussed the saving faith we heard about from your people on board ship and in Georgia," said Charles. "But neither of us have received it. We try to preach it but without success. Is it wrong for us to preach to others that which we do not possess ourselves? Are we being hypocrites?"

"Nay, my brother," the German answered. "Preach faith until you have it. *Truth is never out of order.* Then, because you have it, you will preach faith."

Bohler was favorably impressed with the Wesleys. He included the following paragraph in a letter to Count Zinzendorf:

> I traveled with the two brothers, John and Charles Wesley, from London to Oxford. The elder, John, is a good-natured man; he knew he did not properly believe on the Savior and was willing to be taught. . . . Our mode of believing in the Savior is

so easy to Englishmen that they cannot reconcile themselves to it. If it were a little more artful, they would much sooner find their way into it.

John found it necessary to return to London for several days before visiting his mother. Later, on his way to Salisbury, he stopped over at Oxford again, to find that Charles had developed a cold with a severe cough and acute chest pains. John considered canceling his trip to care for him, but Charles objected strenuously. John left him in the hands of Peter Bohler and some old friends. Then John procured a riding horse and bade them all good-bye.

John reached Salisbury on a gloomy afternoon—one chilly enough that a blazing fire in the hearth added to the serenity of the hour. There mother and son sat once again engaged in serious conversation. John presented anew the spiritual problem that plagued him. Susanna listened with more than ordinary interest. He told her of the embarrassing situation he had fostered during the discussion of the Word with Charles and the Delamottes. He tried to explain the doctrines basic in Moravian philosophy. He asked whether she would agree that the new birth Jesus discussed with Nicodemus might be one and the same as the inward witness his father contended was the strongest proof of Christianity.

John found his mother much more open than before to a theology she had always rejected.

"Ever since you left for America, I have shared your burden," she told him. "Sometimes I fear death and the great unknown. I could not die tonight with the calm tranquility your father possessed to the very moment of his release.

"Son," she said, "St. Peter wrote to the early Christians, saying, 'God is not willing that any should perish.' Upon that assertion I shall stand—serving the Lord to the best of my ability, waiting for the assurance of my salvation. I hope that helps you, John, for it contains everything I have to offer."

Following a long moment of silence, John responded, "I shall seek until I find. I have no other option. And you, dear Mother, shall be among the first to receive my witness. I plan to spend several days with you, then go on to Tiverton to visit Sammy and his family. I hope he receives me with the grace he extended Charles. I have always felt that Sammy doesn't like me."

Susanna faced her son squarely. "John," she said, "that is because Sammy has never felt that you care for him. The time has come for you and your brother to get together for long, unburdening dialogue."

John agreed, but such a meeting had to be delayed. The day before his intended departure, he received a note in the post saying that Charles was ill with a high fever and an unusually severe case of pleurisy. "Please come at once," the missive read. "We fear he is sick unto death."

CHAPTER VIII
Peace

When John reached Oxford, he was happy to learn that his brother had passed the crisis and was on the road to recovery. But Charles felt so weak in body and depressed in spirit that he remained bedfast for many days. Peter Bohler was with him, having stayed by the side of his friend through the long nights and days of his illness.

John wrote to his mother that Charles was improving daily, but except for the constant care and fervent prayer of Mr. Bohler, he might have died.

Susanna read the letter with mixed emotions—happiness for Charles's recovery, concern for John's sagging faith. She was doubly disturbed by the latter owing to her inability to help him. Her secret desire was to meet the Moravian brother who impressed her sons so deeply.

John was experiencing mixed emotions, too. In his association with Peter Bohler, sometimes he really believed that heaven was hearing and answering his prayers. Then dark and ominous doubts would flood his mind and heart until he became convinced of his unbelief. He knew he was not an atheist, but he was unhappy and confused.

In such times, he longed to be like his brother Sammy, who served the Lord and the church so casually that he knew nothing of either the pain or the pleasure of a close relationship with God. John even considered asking to be released from the obligations he assumed in ordination, henceforth to pursue his study of medicine. But his German friend's words, "Preach faith until you have it," kept ringing in his ears.

Bohler became John's confidant. Nothing did he withhold from this good man who had walked into his life that hour of his deepest need.

Bohler seemed to sense the consequential nature of John's peculiar problem. "The Lord may be taking you through great tribulation, preparing you for that which *He knows* lies ahead," Peter explained. "He will supply the faith for which you seek in His own good time. I have a strange feeling that He is trying to tell me that you will preach with unprecedented power and many souls will be saved."

"Someday I shall have lived well enough and long enough to merit the promised grace," John answered weakly.

"Nein!" the German shouted. "You may grow up to it but never into it. When it comes, it will be the free gift of God wrought instantly with such assurance that a thousand imps of hell, together with all the fiends of earth, will not be able to talk you out of it."

One bright, sunny morning, Charles felt well enough to dress himself and take a short walk to help regain his

strength. He hadn't gone far when he met an old acquaintance who had befriended the Holy Club although
he stoutly declined to join it. Wilson Beck was a personable fellow with a flair for the spectacular. Charles remembered him as being a fanatic for reform, openly
critical of both the British Parliament and the king for
failing to deal with the evils of the day.

With him was a small, abnormally thin fellow with a
massive forehead, above which a mop of bushy, black
hair accentuated the unhealthy pallor of his skin. Wilson
introduced his friend. "This is Daniel Dunlevy. You may
have heard of him."

Charles had heard of the controversial man, but he
wisely acknowledged the introduction without saying
so. Then Wilson, in his normal, enthusiastic manner,
explained that Daniel was scheduled to address a group
of interested citizens that evening at a mission meeting-
house they had rented for the occasion. His subject:
"Why Kingdoms Fall."

"Daniel will expose some startling statistics and propose a remedy for our nation's ills which, I think, will be
of special interest to you and John and all your friends,"
said Wilson. "We will be highly honored to have you
attend the lecture."

An hour later, Charles, reclining on his bed, was
surrounded by a half dozen friends including his brother
and Peter Bohler. He told them of meeting Wilson Beck
and his strange companion.

"I recall your deep interest, John, in this Dunlevy
fellow," said Charles. "I'm anxious to hear what you
remember about him."

"Oh, I remember him well," said John. "The last I
heard, he was fast becoming a candidate for the chopping
block. Then he disappeared. Maybe he has had a change

of heart. I'm suggesting that we attend his lecture. He surely can't hurt us."

"Tell us all you know about him," Charles pleaded.

"Well, I'll do the best I can," John answered. "Dan Dunlevy was a prodigy—a boy wonder. It was said that if he hadn't been three times expelled for heresy and insubordination from as many universities, he would have received his degree at the tender age of twelve. His parents both died during a smallpox epidemic when he was three. An uncle, a wealthy dealer in the slave trade, adopted Daniel and took him to his palatial home in London. The uncle, whose wife had died, spent so much time away on business that the strange, headstrong little fellow was reared by servants. They, it was said, would have gladly dropped him in the Thames."

John had the undivided attention of his little audience, as he continued his story.

"By age five, Dan was reading far above the level of those supposed to be his mentors. In fact, at six, he buried himself in the writings of Voltaire, who was promoting revolution in France. The following year, 1726, Voltaire, having served time in the Bastille, came to England. I remember the year, for he arrived soon after I was made Fellow of Lincoln.

"Dunlevy, I think, was about fifteen, pursuing his studies at home. He was bent upon doing in England that which his patron saint was attempting to do in France. For three years, he quietly followed the famous Frenchman, attending his lectures and devouring his books. Then Voltaire returned to Paris.

"As brilliant as Dunlevy was, like most geniuses he had some dangerous blind spots. He threw caution to the winds as he preached one sermon, 'Rebellion of the Masses,' openly with great vigor. He ran into serious trouble immediately, of course. To save his life, his uncle shipped him off to some far shore. He was soon generally forgotten. I haven't heard his name from that day until this.

"Now you fellows know as much about him as I do."

"Perhaps we will know a lot more if we hear him speak," said Charles.

That evening, John and Bohler, assisting Charles, hired a coach to take them to the hall. They arrived a few minutes before the appointed hour to find Wilson Beck and Daniel Dunlevy already seated on the platform. Several hundred people were in attendance.

Wilson arose to greet the audience with a smile broad enough to welcome a gathering of twenty times its size. From his introductory remarks, he seemed to assume the crowd was even larger than that.

"Friends," he began. "We are delighted with this fine group of citizens who have set aside all other obligations tonight to hear one who has traveled the world in quest of an answer to the problem of depressed humanity. What more can I say? Mr. Dunlevy needs no further introduction. His address, long overdue, will answer every question."

Daniel Dunlevy stepped unsteadily to the tiny podium, which he grasped firmly.

"Friends," he began. "My message will be brief and to the point. I need not tell you that the British Empire totters on the brink of disaster with hardly a hope of recovery. Ten years ago, I was ushered out of England under cover of darkness for advocating rebellion as the only solution to our nation's ills.

"The first half of my message is much stronger now

than in those earlier times, for our country's sins are nearly past redemption. From any given point, one may view the horrid panorama of lust, waste, poverty, slavery, child labor, pornography, sodomy, whoredom, drunkenness, abortion, and the utter despair of the masses.

"The last three years of my exile were spent in Frankfurt. There I made an exhaustive study of the rise and fall of nations, whose disgraceful histories followed this same road to destruction. Leaders who refused to listen to their prophets lived to bathe in the blood of their innocent children. That study was stimulated when I crossed the ocean on one of my uncle's slave ships, the horror of which you wouldn't believe if I told you."

Then he pictured at length the unbelievable conditions he had recently beheld in every corner of the commonwealth. The audience was spellbound, wondering in what direction the eloquent orator was about to lead them. The people could see that he was tiring as he hurried to his conclusion.

"There is a way out," he said, dropping his voice and speaking with an intense seriousness that pierced every heart in his hearing. "Only those nations that repented of their sins and experienced spiritual renewal were delivered from chaos. Those revivals each seem to have been centered around an individual whom it is usually assumed was called especially for the task. Among many, consider Francis of Assisi, John Huss, Martin Luther, Savonarola, Calvin and, more recently, John Knox, whose ministry fairly shook the foundation stones of Scotland."

The audience was certain that this former rabble-rouser had turned evangelist, but they were wrong.

"I'm aware that I must sound like a preacher," the strange little fellow said, "but I'm not even a Christian.

I know nothing of experiential religion. I have never taken the time to test it, and I have been disillusioned by a corrupt and often drunken clergy staggering in the streets of our cities. But I know what history teaches from Sodom and Gomorrah to Paris and London. I know what Britain needs in this awful hour.

"I already said that ten years ago I was under indictment for advocating rebellion. If I were forced to face that old charge tonight, it wouldn't matter. I have only months to live. An incurable malady has fastened itself upon my body which, at its best, was never robust.

"Whatever time and strength I am yet allotted is dedicated wholly to the task of unveiling the facts of our nation's depravity, together with history's only hope for restoration. This is my atonement for the mistakes of a misdirected youth. I ask for no man's money. I still have ample *tainted* funds from my late uncle's slave-trading ventures, which I gladly appropriate for the cause I represent. My sole request is for assistance in procuring opportunities to present my message. Mr. Beck is helping me. If you have suggestions, please talk with him."

He was through, but he clung silently to the podium until Wilson assisted him to a chair. Peter Bohler stepped up quickly to address the speaker. John and Charles heard him say in his native tongue: "You spent three years in Frankfurt. Do you speak German?"

"Fluently," Dunlevy answered.

"Good. May I visit you on the morrow?"

The Wesleys saw an affirmative nod, but that was all. Peter Bohler never talked of his evangelistic efforts or bragged about his converts. Several weeks later, though, John was told of Dunlevy's peaceful passing.

John and Charles discussed the meeting late into the night, which was contrary to their general practice. They were deeply ashamed of their own feeble efforts to do the work to which they supposed they had been called. Then their conversation shifted, as it was prone to do, to the question of instantaneous conversion.

"Last night in my devotions," said John, "I was the most miserable of men. I cried out in desperation, 'Lord, help my unbelief!' But I felt no response to what I felt was earnest prayer. You know, Charles, if only I could witness one sinner saved by grace alone, I believe my faith would make me whole."

In the following incident, John's first wish was granted, but the pragmatic request was still unanswered.

A condemned prisoner, awaiting execution at the *Castle,* had twice been visited by Peter Bohler. Speaking to John and a friend, Charles Kinchin, Peter explained that the poor fellow could not understand his broken English.

"Perhaps, John, if you were to go to him and present the claims of Christ, he might yet accept the gift of life."

John was hesitant. To preach at the *Castle* was one thing, but to sit down face-to-face with a man about to die and talk of a saving grace he had never found for himself was quite another. Then Kinchin broke into the conversation to explain that time was running out for the prisoner.

"This is his last full day upon earth," he stated sadly. "Tomorrow he must die. I plan to visit him this afternoon, but I have no words or talent to lead the poor soul to Christ."

"Go with him, John!" Bohler nearly shouted. "Speak that faith you have been preaching and pray for the man's salvation."

John could not refuse the earnest plea. At the *Castle,*

he and Kinchin were ushered to a gloomy, smelly cell with one small window high above their heads. On an old, rough bench, the derelict sat with head bowed—face hidden in his hands—moaning in despair.

Kinchin sat down beside him and placed a loving arm around his shoulders. John opened his Bible and steeled himself to his task. The tempter was whispering, "Don't do it, John. It will condemn your soul and render no good to the one who deserves to die." The satanic message seemed valid as the voice came through loud and clear. John weighed it against the words of Peter Bohler: "Preach faith until you have it. . . ."

I may lose my soul, John mused in terror, *but I will have tried to save another. Perhaps God will honor that.*

"Don't do it," cried the tempter.

Then the prisoner raised his head to stare straight into the eyes of the man with the Bible. That did it. The simple words that followed may well have been one of the greatest sermons John Wesley ever preached.

"My friend," John spoke softly. "We have come to tell you that God is not willing that any should perish. The Bible says, 'Come now, and let us reason together. . . . Though your sins be as scarlet, they shall be as white as snow.'

"Listen to these simple words of truth: 'For all have sinned and come short of the glory of God. . . . For the wages of sin is death, but the gift of God is eternal life through Jesus Christ our Lord. . . . For by grace are ye saved through faith; and that not of yourselves: it is the gift of God: not of works, lest any man should boast. . . . Repent ye therefore, and be converted, that your sins may be blotted out. . . . God is love.'"

The man listened with rapt attention, reaching for every syllable, every sound. John saw a deep concern, a sense of sorrow, and a ray of hope shine through the brightening countenance of the convicted felon who was beginning to exercise a childlike faith in the Man of Sorrows.

"Hear these prayers," spoke John in his best pulpit manner. But after reading several lines from the prayer book he always carried with his Bible, he sensed the futility of confronting God with petitions penned by another in centuries past. He closed the book and launched out in earnest, fervent, impromptu prayer, interceding for a lost soul. His words began to flow, surprising himself and melting the hearts of the men before him. The condemned man reached for the preacher's hand as he fell to his knees, weeping like a boy. The enemy's struggle for his soul had been long and strong, but the repentant heart claimed Jesus. Another name was added to the Book of Life.

The prisoner raised his head as he brushed away his tears with a rough, bony fist. Speaking gratefully with deep conviction, he said, "I am ready now to die. Jesus has taken away my sins."

The following morning his emaciated body was dropped to its death by hanging. But John and Kinchin, who stayed with the prisoner to the last, knew that his soul had gone to God. And John Wesley had crossed a bridge toward his future destination as God's evangelist.

(It was said that John, who had always read his prayers using a collect or two followed by the Lord's Prayer, thereafter prayed with or without a form as suited the occasion.)

Following the execution, John went to visit Charles. He described the prison experience in detail. "I was amazed," he said, "at the divine drama being enacted before my eyes. You remember that I once said my faith would make me whole if I could witness an instantaneous conversion. Charles, even this conversion did not give me personal faith."

"During my illness, John, I did a lot of thinking. Can it be that we have depended so much on knowledge that we haven't been able to cast ourselves on simple grace?"

"I'm listening, Charles."

"Could it be that there has been too much of Wesley and not enough of God? Or perhaps too much of God in general; too little of Christ in particular? Or do you think, John, that Peter Bohler could have been right when he suggested that God may be leading you through great tribulation in preparation for something He knows lies ahead?

"I didn't give that a second thought," said John. "But when I heard Dan Dunlevy, who claimed no knowledge of grace, plead for revival until there was hardly a dry eye in his audience, I'll have to admit that my heart was stirred within me."

"Are you prepared to accept the will of God, whatever it may encompass?" Charles asked.

"Are you?" John countered.

"I don't know where I stand," Charles answered thoughtfully. "When I was ill, I felt very close to the kingdom. But now that I am up and about again, I fear I'm losing ground."

After John departed, Charles sat alone in earnest contemplation. John's description of the felon's faith as he faced the gallows impressed him deeply. The simplicity of it appealed to him, but he knew not how to grasp it. He longed to put it into verse, to sing it with his friends, to shout it to the world. But he sensed his unworthiness.

"What license have I to sing or write or preach?" he asked himself, bowing his head in utter defeat. Then, a sharp pain pierced him like a sabre—first in his chest, then through to his back. It nearly doubled him over; the pangs of pleurisy were harassing him.

John, hearing his call, assisted him to a cot, where he lay in deep distress.

"I'll have someone fix a bed for you at once," said John.

"No," Charles gasped. "I want to be taken to the home of Mr. Bray."

"But why?" asked John. "Bray is an ignorant tradesman who admits he knows nothing but the Lord. The poor fellow's house is old and drafty. His beds are probably hard as iron slabs."

"But, John, I haven't told you everything. In my daily meditation, I was reminded of Saul of Tarsus. He was a much greater sinner than I." Charles, gasping for breath, paused a few moments until the pain relaxed. "He was better educated, too, and certainly more successful in his chosen field. Nevertheless, some time after his conversion, he went into Corinth saying, 'I am determined not to know anything among you, save Jesus Christ, and him crucified.' He became like Bray, don't you see? Somewhere in all this there must be an answer to my prayers. Please take me to Mr. Bray." The request was honored. He was taken to the humble home of his friend where loving care and effectual prayer were his without asking.

Two days later, alone in meditation, Charles Wesley reached up in faith to touch the nail-scarred hands of Jesus. Even the pleurisy fled with the burden of sin.

Joy unspeakable and full of glory! Charles put new words to old melodies—new love, new inspiration, and great new meaning to familiar truths:

> *Finish then thy new creation*
> *Pure and spotless let us be;*
> *Let us see our whole salvation*
> *Perfectly restored in thee.*
> —*Charles Wesley*

John, unaware of Charles's commitment, was more deeply distressed than ever with his own inability to find that elusive, promised peace for himself. He attended a worship service at St. Mary-le-Strand to hear his friend Dr. Heylyn deliver the Word. This popular, talented minister was delighted to see John in his congregation. He called upon him to assist with the sacrament.

Following the service, a gentleman whom John would later recall only vaguely approached him with the news that Charles had accepted Christ as Savior. John could hardly have been happier for his brother's sake, but the news only deepened his own distress. His first impulse was to go immediately to hear Charles's own account of his new birth, hoping thus to be led through the door to his own salvation. He quickly decided against it, however, for fear the utter darkness that now enveloped him—mind and spirit—might dampen the ardor and destroy the ecstasy of Charles's triumphant hour.

John wandered from place to place that day, trying in vain to do some little good. The following morning, he opened his Bible and read, "There are given unto us exceeding great and precious promises." He closed the book and walked the lonely streets again. In the afternoon, he made his way to St. Paul's Cathedral where he listened to the anthem, "Out of the deep have I called unto thee, O Lord . . . O Israel, trust in the Lord, for with the Lord there is mercy, and with Him is plenteous redemption. And He shall redeem Israel from all His sins."

Into the streets again, the problem-laden preacher carried the burden of unforgiven sins. At eventide, he stood alone by the ancient wall and watched the shadows of the city prepare to die with the dying sun. As the black night fell, he watched the eerie glow of wicks and tapers begin to dot the darkness all around him. He moved on into Aldersgate Street where he fell into conversation with a man who was on his way to attend a mission. They walked together until they stood before the open door of a dimly lighted room.

"Come in with me," the other suggested, but John was hesitant. Inside, a lay leader was having difficulty reading Luther's *Introduction to the Book of Romans*. John believed that only men of the cloth should be permitted leadership in such a meeting. Then he was reminded of Charles and Mr. Bray, the tradesman who knew nothing but Christ and Him crucified. John quietly took a seat on a rough homemade bench just inside the door and tried to listen. The reader continued, coming to the lines describing the miraculous change that is wrought by God in the hearts of believers. Suddenly a light—not the dim flicker of a penny candle, but a hallowed glow of love and mercy—began to shine.

John stated later: "I felt my heart strangely warmed. I felt that I did trust in Christ, Christ alone, for salvation: An assurance was given me that he had taken away my sin, even mine, and saved me from the law of sin and death!

> *How happy is my pilgrim's lot.*
> *How free from every anxious thought.*
> *This happiness in part is mine*
> *Already saved from low design.*
> *My soul is lightened of its load*
> *And seeks the things above.*
> —*John Wesley*

CHAPTER IX

Revive Thy Church, O Lord

Rev. Benjamin Ingham arose from his bed one morning in February 1739, a bit depressed and with no particular plans for the day. But at breakfast this all changed. He was informed that his old friend, Charles Delamotte, was back in England, visiting his family at Bixley. The twenty eventful months these two young men had spent in Georgia assisting the Wesleys were fresh in his mind.

Ben penned a note of warmest welcome, suggesting they meet that afternoon at an address on Fetter Lane where they could visit without distraction. The note was delivered by courier late that morning. Delamotte was delighted.

That afternoon, the two friends entered a hall that had been turned into a chapel. Scores of chairs were strewn in disorderly fashion, and the floor was ready for the broom. Ingham smiled at the startled expression on the face of his friend.

"This is the meeting place of the Fetter Lane Society," Ben explained. "A love feast was held here last night. Apparently no one has gotten around to put the room in order."

"I see what you mean by a quiet place where there will be no distractions," said Delamotte, smiling at his own bit of humor. "But just what is this Fetter Lane Society?"

"It is a fellowship that was organized by a Moravian named Peter Bohler," Ben explained. "Peter is now on his way to America, but you'll be hearing more about him. Largely through his influence, John and Charles finally found the peace for which they had been searching. You'll be hearing more about that, too. The members of Bohler's little society agreed to meet every week. They formed themselves into small bands to make it easy to speak freely with one another about their religious life. A love feast was established in which all members meet on a Sunday evening once a month from seven to ten."

"I presume it is a rather exclusive club," remarked Delamotte.

"Yes, it is," Ingham answered. "All who wish to join must remain on trial for two months."

"Has it been an effective means of grace, Ben?"

"It surely has been that," said Ingham. "It was here that Charles Wesley, in earnest conversation with Bohler, was convinced—in mind, that is—of the true nature of evangelical faith. Soon after that, Bohler embarked for Carolina."

"What about John?" asked Delamotte. "How much has he been influenced by this man, Bohler?"

"More than you can guess," answered Ingham. "I'll not presume to give testimony for him. He will be taking care of that himself—and soon, you may be sure. I might give a little hint, though, by repeating something I heard him say last night."

"Do it, by all means," said Delamotte. "If John said it, I want to hear it."

"As nearly as I can recall," Ingham continued, "it went like this: 'Oh what a work has God begun since Peter Bohler came into England. It is such as shall never come to an end till heaven and earth pass away.'

"The Fetter Lane Society has grown from four to forty members, with many more attending the meetings," Ingham boasted. "At least sixty—including the Wesleys, Whitefield, Wesley Hall, Kinchin, Hutchins, myself, and others you have known—met here last New Year's Eve for a love feast and all-night prayer vigil. The pubs, of course, were bursting with business, but we had a celebration that put those dens to shame. Much of the night was spent in prayer for the salvation of the thousands of sinners engaged in drunken brawls across the city. The meeting progressed far into the night with prayers, testimonies, and exhortations continuing without a break."

Then, coming to his feet, Ingham spoke excitedly: "Suddenly we received a visitation from heaven so unexpected and earthshaking that I can't possibly describe it." He paused in an effort to control his emotions. "I tell you, God poured out His Spirit upon us in such measure and power that it could have been nothing less than a reenactment of Pentecost. It seemed as though Christ Himself were standing in our midst, saying, 'Receive ye power to be witnesses unto me in all Britain, on the continent, America, and to the uttermost part of the earth.'"

Ben paced the floor. "I was hoping that some of the glory might be lingering here today," he continued. "I'm

117

sorry if I have made this sound incredible, but I owe it to the Lord to share it with everyone I meet."

"Oh, I understand," Delamotte answered, also rising from his chair. "After seeing the change that has taken place in my family—especially in Mother—I can believe anything. Father has mellowed beyond belief, and those brothers of mine haven't argued or fought one time since I've been home. I can hardly believe it."

He began slowly to put the chairs in order. "Ben, I guess you know I haven't experienced this new birth." Then, trying to hide his embarrassment, he continued, "But when I'm convinced it is for me, I shall seek it."

Ingham smiled. "Delamotte, 'You are not far from the kingdom,'" he quoted.

"Ben, I'm confused. I always had great respect for John Wesley. When he said that one must keep all the ordinances of God to get to heaven, I believed him. I've never been able to live that well, but the Moravians couldn't change my mind. Now you make it sound as though John has cast aside his old convictions. What *does* he believe?"

Ingham chose his words carefully. "John and Charles have both come to trust in Christ alone for their salvation. That is now paramount in their preaching. I would say that they have simply added a new dimension to their theology. They contend for holiness of heart and life as strongly as ever.

"Immediately following their conversions, John spent several weeks in Germany visiting Count Zinzendorf and observing his people. I would say that his respect for the Moravians is as strong as ever, but beyond the born-again experience, he quietly disagrees with some of their teaching and way of life. You may be sure, though, there is nothing contentious or critical in his attitude."

Delamotte was listening intently, weighing every word. "What about Charles?" he asked.

"While John was gone, Charles kept on preaching to growing crowds wherever pulpits were open to him," Ingham answered. "The churches couldn't begin to hold the people. His preaching was much too evangelistic, however, to suit the rectors. Many of them would not allow him to return. Soon after John arrived back from Germany, practically every door was closed to them."

"Tell me, Ben. Since John and Charles are both ordained priests of the established church, should the rectors refuse them the right to preach in their pulpits?"

"Some of the Wesleys' friends are more critical than I," said Ingham. "There are serious problems involved."

"What kind of problems, Ben?"

"Well, the State Church is a rather sophisticated organism, as you know. The rectors are subject to ecclesiastical authority as well as to the reactions of their members. Granted, most of the people are spiritually cold and indifferent to whatever may go on outside the church, but within it, they expect order and finesse."

"Shouldn't they, Ben?"

"I think so," Ingham answered. "John and Charles agree. High Church etiquette is all they've ever known. Whitefield is deeply disturbed by the trouble, for the doors are closing to him as well. But the present problem is one they cannot handle."

"What is it?" Delamotte asked.

"Most people call it enthusiasm," said Ingham. "Many of the people pouring into the services haven't been inside a church for years. They've suffered every kind of hardship, every kind of bondage. They are steeped in sin. The gospel as John and Charles and George are preaching it—"know the truth, and the truth shall make you free"—is the best news these depressed, forgotten souls have ever heard. They live in fear, and their greatest fear is death—satanic fire. They know *that's* in the Bible."

"Go on," said Delamotte. "I want it all."

"When they hear that Jesus loves them—suffered more than they—and died on a cross to give them life," Ben continued, "they cast away all doubts and take Him at His word. The release from sin and Satan is so startling that these people can't resist shouting it to the world. Such demonstration is especially strong under John's preaching. That's a bit strange, for everyone agrees that Charles and Whitefield are better preachers than he. But Whitefield says, 'When John throws back his head and begins to expound the Word, the very gates of hell tremble on their hinges.'

"Women scream, men weep, and I've seen sinners fall prostrate in the aisles and lie as dead. A few moments later they arise and shout praises unto God."

"Amazing," whispered Delamotte.

"Another problem came upon the heels of the first one," Ingham continued. "Counterfeiters appeared, mimicking the converts—some simply wanting attention, others hoping for gain. John answers the critics, saying, 'No one counterfeits anything but that which is genuine.' Most critics claim it is all of the devil, but John rebukes them, asking, 'Does the devil save souls?'"

The men, tired of standing, resumed their seats as Ben continued: "No one denies that lives are being changed by the hundreds. Satan is being defeated on every hand. These converts cease their drinking and refuse to use the name of God in vain. Making restitution has become the talk of the town. Wife beating, burglaries, rape, and other licentious acts are dropping to an all-time low.

"And it isn't only the poor that receive the Gospel.

Affluent, highly respected families like your own are being saved. We hear of slaves being freed and wages raised. New reforms are being written for Parliament to consider.

"John is as deeply disturbed by the enthusiasm as anyone. But he says, 'As long as God is transforming lives, we must not lay a hand upon it. Just leave it with the Lord.'"

"Did you say that all church doors are closed against the evangelists?" asked Delamotte.

"Yes, but they continue to preach in halls like this, in private homes, in empty buildings—anywhere they can—two and three times a day. The crowds keep coming. Whitefield has gone to Bristol, where he preached before going to Georgia. He felt sure the churches there would receive him."

"What about you, Ben?"

Ingham took a long breath and relaxed a bit before answering. "The Lord seems to have given me a ministry of reconciliation," he said. "Everyone knows that I endorse the revival, but I am not an evangelist in the same sense as John and the others. That bothered me at first, but Charles and I had a long talk that helped me. 'Don't mimic anyone,' was Charles's advice. 'Just be yourself and follow the leading of the Spirit.' He went on to say that the Lord had a special ministry for him, too—that he would always be walking in John's shadow. 'The Lord needed Andrew as well as Peter,' he concluded.

"Since then I have been happy in my work. I have discovered that many of the ministers in the churches believe the rising moral tide is the direct result of the awakening. They are glad to have me calmly explain this to their people without upsetting the services. I'll wait for my reward in heaven."

"You may not be an evangelist, Ben, but you're the most convincing fellow I ever met," said Delamotte seriously. "Almost thou persuadest me to be a Christian."

For a long half hour, the two men visited, reliving their days in Georgia. Then Delamotte, who could always read his friend when trouble lurked in the shadows, asked a pointed question:

"What is on your mind, Ben? I sense that something is bothering you."

"You're right," Ben answered. "It has to do with Sam Wesley in Tiverton. He and John have never gotten along very well. Now Sammy, who always had a quick temper, is almost beside himself with rage over exaggerated reports of these meetings. He blames John. A few radical newspapers have been strongly opposing the revival, highlighting the enthusiasm. One paper published an artist's drawing of a teenage girl falling dead in her mother's arms. Another claimed that murder had been committed in the chancel of a church in London. Tragically, Sammy's mother is taking the brunt of Sammy's burning criticism. She had mixed emotions regarding these reports herself."

"How does this involve you?" asked Delamotte.

"Charles confided in me," said Ben. "He is deeply disturbed, of course. He said that John had written their mother a long letter of explanation, which she accepted very well. She shared it with a friend who gave it to Sammy. He in turn wrote Susanna a scorching indictment of John's participation in what he called 'all this disgraceful frenzy.' In it, he misquoted lines from John's letter so radically that his mother didn't recognize their source.

"George Whitefield and John have both visited Susanna," Ben went on. "She is convinced now that the revival is of God, but that doesn't help Sammy. From early childhood, Charles was Sammy's favorite sibling. Charles would like to visit his brother, but being so deeply involved in the awakening, he fears a confrontation would make matters worse."

"I can understand that," said Delamotte. "But, except for a natural interest in your friend's affairs, I still don't see how you are included in the problem."

"Charles has asked me to visit Sammy," Ingham explained. "He says my call to a ministry of reconciliation prepares me for the task."

"How do you feel about it, Ben?"

"Certainly not at ease," he answered. "Sammy doesn't know me very well, but he must be aware that I am involved in the meetings with John and Charles. My fear is that he will resent my interfering in a family affair. And he will probably assume I am there to try to convert him."

"Yes, Ben, I think you are right," said Delamotte. "I'm sure you would find yourself in a most awkward position. Give me a few moments to think about it. Maybe I can help you."

For some little time, the two men sat in quiet contemplation, then Delamotte continued slowly: "When Sammy lived in Westminster, he was friendly with my family. I was rather young then, but I remember him well. I think he liked me. Perhaps I'm the one to visit him. I can tell him honestly that I am not a part of the strange phenomenon that is causing such a stir across the land. And he will be pleased to learn that I have not entered into the conversion experience its advocates are preaching. If I'm careful, I may have good fellowship with him."

"Will you try?" begged Ingham.

"Not until I have talked with John and Charles, of course. But if they agree, I will do my best. Would it be possible, Ben, for you and John and Charles to spend tomorrow night with me at Bixley? My family would be delighted, and it will be like old times for you and me. Discussion around the fire throughout the long winter evening should be a pleasure. Father will allow me to take you home in his rig the next morning."

"I'll arrange it if I can," said Ben. "You may be sure of that."

The evening at the Delamottes' could hardly have been improved upon. John and Charles, after preaching steadily for weeks, needed the diversion more than they realized. For more than an hour, Charles sat at the organ, leading the others in singing psalms and introducing the verses he had been writing. Mr. Delamotte read Paul's letter to Timothy from the family Bible and each in turned prayed and praised the Lord. Mrs. Delamotte was the perfect hostess, arranging for refreshments to be served at exactly the proper time. John, at the request of the group, gave a short exhortation, emphasizing the importance of Christians "going on to perfection."

"Don't let this confuse you," he said. "Seek for nothing but more of the love of God."

Charles Delamotte, sticking close to his friend Ben Ingham, entered into the spirit of the meeting with ease and pleasure. Everyone present was aware that he—a beloved son—was, in a sense, the one outsider of the group, but nothing was said to suggest it.

The next morning after a hearty breakfast, Delamotte hitched a team of spirited geldings to his father's handsome, two-seated rig and delivered the three friends to their respective homes. On the way they discussed at length the Wesleys' problem involving their brother Sammy. Delamotte's offer to visit him received unanimous approval.

Several days later, Delamotte saddled his favorite riding horse and started out for Tiverton. A light snowfall during the night had turned the English countryside into a land of sparkling beauty, adding much to the pleasure of the trip. Allowing the steed to choose its stride, Delamotte rode along in quiet contemplation. He could only guess how he might be received at the end of his long journey. He didn't worry, but he wondered.

Midway between London and Tiverton stood the village of Salisbury, where Susanna Wesley was making her home temporarily. Having gotten an early start, Delamotte hoped to reach this halfway point by late afternoon. John and Charles had insisted on his visiting their mother before trying to get an audience with Sammy, for her advice would be invaluable.

The winter sun was setting when the weary rider reached Salisbury. Susanna, having met Delamotte on a couple of occasions, was delighted when she saw him standing at her door. She welcomed him as an old friend of the family.

Actually, Susanna had more in common with this meticulous young man, who had been a dutiful disciple of John's, than with any of her own three sons. He had absorbed her legalistic views through John in Georgia. He, like Susanna, had not yet accepted the new dimension in John's theology. Susanna Wesley at the ripening age of sixty-nine and Charles Delamotte, a youth of twenty-four, found much indeed to talk about through the long winter evening. How Delamotte might meet Sammy with some degree of cordiality finally became foremost in their discussion.

"Sammy inherited a few of his father's strongest traits," explained Susanna. "The stubborn attitude he is taking toward his brothers now is one of them. I have had to deal with it most of my life," she added. Delamotte caught the touch of a smile in her eyes, although her lips divulged no hint of any hidden emotion. "Past experiences," she went on to say, "will help me now in writing a note to prepare him for your visit. I have friends leaving for Tiverton in the morning. They will deliver it.

"You must remain here for a couple of days," she instructed. "By then, I'm quite sure Sammy will be ready to receive you with respect."

The note—a masterpiece of diplomacy—said she was entertaining a most delightful young guest, Charles Delamotte. She reminded Sammy that he had known the Delamottes of Bixley when he lived in Westminster. Their son, she explained, is a good friend of John and Charles but was concerned about their present activities.

She concluded, "He wishes to talk with you. I'm suggesting that he ride on to Tiverton. You will enjoy his fellowship. He plans to arrive there Friday evening. God bless you."

Delamotte tied his horse at a hitching post in front of Blondell's School, where Sammy Wesley served as headmaster. A few students came out of the building into the chilly air, wrapping their coats about themselves. It appeared that classes were over for the day.

Once inside, Delamotte made his way to the headmaster's office. The door was open. Sammy was at his desk, finishing his work for the week. He looked up and saw his guest standing in the doorway.

"Charles Delamotte!" he cried, smiling his welcome, as he arose from his chair. "Come in, come in. I remember you as a teenage lad."

"Thank you, Mr. Wesley," said Delamotte, taking a proffered hand. "I recall your visits to our home in Bixley. That seems like a long, long time ago."

Sammy was handsome, strong, and mature, giving the impression of being rich and important but not at all conceited or aloof. Delamotte liked him, noting how much he resembled his brothers, although he appeared larger, much older, and perhaps less venturesome than they.

"Come," said Sammy, reaching for his coat. "I'll walk you to my home. It isn't far. My wife is expecting you for dinner." At the outer door the gracious host saw his visitor's horse tethered at the gate. "I have a barn," he said. "Bring your steed along. We'll feed him and bed him down for the night. I have a team of fillies in a stall by themselves. They will cause no problem."

Sammy's wife met them at the door. She remembered the Delamottes, too. No formal introduction was necessary. "It is nice to have a young guest," she said seriously. "Our family is grown and gone. I hope you'll stay for a good, long visit."

Sammy took his friend to an elaborate guest room.

"The last one to occupy this facility," he said, "was Alexander Pope. I have been singularly blessed with the acquaintances of several famous poets."

"I didn't know I would be so highly honored," said Delamotte. "The nearest I have come to knowing a real poet personally has been in my association with your brother Charles. His verses are excellent, but they, of course, are cast in a different mold than those of Mr. Pope."

"Charles lived with us from the time he was eight until he entered Oxford," said Sammy. "His talent began to show very early. I was getting poems published at that time and had been invited to join a rather exclusive club. It turned out that I was not in a class with the other members, but they became my friends. Our home in Westminster was a convenient meeting place for the group. Charles got to know Pope, Addison, Swift, and many others. I'm sure they were an inspiration to him."

After a sumptuous evening meal of beef ribs baked in a rich brown sauce, Sammy and Delamotte retired to the den—Wesley's private library and study. When they were comfortably seated, Sammy opened the subject of the revival.

"I guess you know I've been deeply disturbed by the reports of John's disgusting activities," he began.

"Your mother told me that," Delamotte answered honestly.

"She sent me a note saying you are troubled, too," said Sammy.

"I guess you can say that," Delamotte felt he was walking a tightrope as he proceeded carefully. "Up to this point, at least, I have been unable to accept the new birth theory that your brothers and Mr. Whitefield are contending for. It seems they have been influenced by the German Moravians."

"I know something about that," said Sammy. "My father always claimed an inward witness that gave him the assurance of salvation. I never allowed that to bother me. What does bother me is that the poor and ignorant are subscribing to such an experience and reacting with wild, disgraceful antics that the devil himself might abhor."

Sammy reached for a newssheet that lay on his desk. He pointed to the drawing of the girl falling dead in her mother's arms. "This came while Mr. Pope was with us," he cried. "Can you imagine my embarrassment?" Sammy's face flushed pink as his anger mounted. "The next day I was the laughingstock of the town. Even the students looked at me and grinned with amusement. What could I say with my own brother responsible for the whole unbelievable affair?"

"I sense your problem keenly," said Delamotte, "for I have had to face it, too. But the reports have been exaggerated. No deaths or even injuries have occurred. The enthusiasm in the meetings is terribly embarrassing to the preachers. It happens in Charles's and Whitefield's meetings as well as John's. None of the men know how to deal with it."

Sammy laid the paper aside. "You have relieved my mind more than you know," he said. "But why is it that only poor, ignorant people respond to the preaching if it has any basis in truth?"

"That again, sir, is a false report," said Delamotte carefully. "That is what bothers me. It strikes home in my case as well as yours, you see."

"What do you mean?" asked Sammy.

"Well," said Delamotte. "Hardly is there a more highly sophisticated, Anglican family to be found than my own. And they—with the exception of myself, you understand—are witnessing publicly that Christ has forgiven their sins and prepared them for heaven. I daresay they are gathered around the hearth right now, praying for their unsaved son."

"I can only believe that," said Sammy thoughtfully, "because I know you wouldn't lie, especially about a matter as delicate as this."

The two men sat engrossed in silent meditation for several minutes. Then Sammy spoke again:

"I shall write to John, telling him that, while I neither understand nor condone all that I am hearing about this strange new ministry, I must ask him to forgive me for the things I said before I talked with you. And I'll send a copy of the letter to Mother."

Charles Delamotte went to bed that night in the elaborate guest room where some of England's great poets had been entertained. He had mixed emotions regarding his spiritual condition, but for the moment he was at peace with himself. He had accomplished his mission.

CHAPTER X
Look on the Fields

After a hard, sixty-mile ride from Oxford, George Whitefield rode into Bristol. He was happy, for he had scores of friends in this ancient, bustling city of commerce and finance. A warm February sun was setting; early spring was in the air. Whether it would remain was questionable, of course, but for the present everyone was in good spirits.

Located near the mouth of the river Avon, Bristol was an important seaport city. It benefited in great measure from the manufacture and export of tobacco products and the infamous African slave trade to which only the Quakers objected. Coal mining was a lucrative enterprise for the wealthy owners. Labor was so cheap that the working class was extremely poor and ripe for revolution.

The lone horseman, riding into town that evening, was ready for revival. Before his conversion, Whitefield had preached in nearly all of Bristol's churches. He had been extremely popular. Since then, however, exaggerated, adverse reports of the spiritual awakening in London had reached Bristol, where antagonism was raised as it had been in Tiverton. No pastor, much as he may have loved and appreciated the evangelist in the past, dared open his pulpit to Whitefield now. It appeared that he had no place to preach.

Fortunately, the High Church prejudices that hampered the Wesleys were unknown to Whitefield. He could preach the gospel anywhere a congregation might assemble. Jesus had preached on the mountainside and the seashore—why not George Whitefield?

Whitefield, having discovered a mound outside the city on which he could stand, announced that he would preach. A small crowd gathered, mostly out of curiosity. But the prince of orators had a startled audience clinging to his words from the outset. The freedom of the great out-of-doors gave him inspiration and liberty he had never known before. He finished his address in a flurry of excitement.

"I'll preach again," he cried, announcing the hour.

The people—mostly miners and their families—hurried to spread the news. Long before the appointed time, a crowd began to appear. Whitefield saw the gathering from a distance and hurried back to ask whether the people had misunderstood the announcement.

"No," they assured him. "We're being sure we will be close enough to hear you."

"Couldn't you hear me before?" he asked.

"Oh yes," they cried. "But this time the field will be filled with people."

Three men, carrying tools, approached the preacher. "Sir," they said, "we want to build you a higher place to stand. Then you will be heard at greater distance."

"I appreciate what you're doing," said the astonished Whitefield, "but I fear you're being overly optimistic."

How wrong he was. At least two thousand men, women, and children poured onto the green meadow for that second service.

The preacher was at his evangelistic best, exposing sin in a language the most illiterate soul could understand. He pictured "outer darkness" in Jesus' own descriptive terms. In his conclusion, forgiveness, heaven, love, and peace—the precious promises of God—were offered freely to those who believed His Word. From time to time, cries for mercy and tears of repentance nearly broke up the meeting. Revival had come to Bristol.

John and Charles were preaching in halls and hostels—any place they dared to call a church. Unprecedented crowds followed them wherever they preached. For a lack of room to congregate, the greater number of worshipers were turned away disappointed and sometimes disillusioned. By the end of March, a change in pattern was inevitable.

Whitefield was a great preacher, more gifted than either of the Wesleys, but he had little talent for organization. His converts were without church homes, pastors, teachers, or anyone to give them direction. No fellowship of believers existed to receive them into its loving arms. The established churches would not allow these enthusiastic, testifying, newborn believers to cross their thresholds.

Sensing the futility of his efforts, Whitefield decided wisely to turn the Bristol project to another who might establish a foundation for its future. Anyway, his purpose in returning to England had been to raise funds for the construction of an orphanage in Savannah. He needed to get to London where this might be accomplished.

John Wesley was the only one he knew whom he believed could successfully succeed him at Bristol. But he had serious doubts that this dignified, evangelical Anglican priest, clinging to his High Church principles, would agree to hold services in the open air. Whitefield had heard him say that the church was the place to preach.

Letters from both John and Charles convinced him also that they were satisfied with their efforts in London. Ministering two and three times a day in small, inadequate, packed-out halls and houses that had been turned into sanctuaries of sorts fulfilled their calling—so they believed.

"Converts in every service is surely God's stamp of approval upon our labors," they wrote.

Whitefield agreed—with reservation. *If God be pleased with small successes,* he mused, *why would He not be happier with larger ones?* Then he penned a most convincing letter to John.

"You must come," he pleaded. "'The fields are white unto harvest.' God needs you. I need you. These precious people need you. Please do not delay!"

Should he go? John and Charles prayed in vain for an answer from heaven. They presented the problem at Fetter Lane without success. Finally, they resorted to the Moravian practice of drawing straws to reach an elusive mind of the Lord. This method was used in choosing Matthias to replace the traitor, but heaven alone will reveal whether God resorts to this method of conveying His pleasure. Anyway, this fifty-fifty chance of doing His will tipped the scale in Whitefield's favor. John saddled his horse and rode to Bristol.

On Sunday, April 1, 1739, John Wesley stood in his friend's congregation on Bristol's bowling green. Conflicting emotions possessed him as he listened to the Word and witnessed the reactions of the multitude. Later, he wrote the following account of his feelings:

> I could scarce reconcile myself at first to this strange way of preaching in the fields, of which he [Whitefield] set me an example; having all my life (till very lately) so tenacious of every point relating to decency and order, that I should have thought the saving of souls almost a sin if it had not been done in a church.

At the close of that service, Whitefield bade his friend good-bye, left him in charge of the revival, and rode off to London.

John began his work that evening, meeting with a small group in Nicholas Street, where he initiated himself to field preaching by expounding the Sermon on the Mount.

At four the following afternoon, he preached his first out-of-door sermon in the field where Whitefield had begun his ministry. He was amazed to see the hordes of worshipers pour onto the green until a congregation of well over two thousand souls waited impatiently to hear eternal truths from the lips of another preacher.

John opened his Bible and read from the fourth chapter of Luke: "The Spirit of the Lord is upon me, because he hath anointed me to preach the gospel to the poor."

He looked out upon his congregation, thrust his head upward in a typical gesture, causing his long wavy locks to fall back on his narrow shoulders. His sharp, resonant voice had a carrying quality that reached his listeners even on the periphery of the mammoth circle. More important, the little minister possessed a dynamic, inexplicable personality that made him, not the greatest, but one of the most effective preachers in the history of the Christian church. This, no doubt, added fuel to the fire of enthusiasm that he abhorred but knew not how to handle.

The penitent form or inquiry room that later became popular in evangelistic services was unheard of in Wesley's time. The altar call—if indeed one could call it that—was profound in its simplicity. While in the process of preaching, the evangelist would often cry out after the manner of John the Baptist: "Repent! The kingdom of God is at hand!" Counseling the penitent was an integral part of every discourse: "'Ye must be born again.' Christ shed His blood to save you from your sins. Cast away your doubts. Bow your heads and hearts. Accept Him, and Him alone, as Lord and Savior. 'Believe on the Lord Jesus Christ and thou shalt be saved. . . .' Go forth to serve Him with all your heart and mind and soul and strength, and love your neighbor as yourself."

Showers of blessings, shouts of praise, tears of joy nearly broke up the meetings.

John threw himself into the revival with neither hesitation nor reservation. He read prayers each morning at Newgate. On Monday afternoons, he preached out-of-doors near Bristol. Every other Tuesday he went to the sophisticated resort town and health spa of Bath to preach. Wednesdays he held services at Baptist Mills, and alternate Thursdays at Pensford. Friday usually found him preaching in yet another part of Kingswood, and Saturday at Bowling Green. He scheduled at least three services every Sunday.

"Oh, how God has renewed my strength!" he cried. "Ten years ago, I was faint and weary with preaching only two times in one day."

Preaching, however, was only a part of John's huge responsibility. How to nurture his converts was on his mind continually. They were loosely divided into societies—a step in the right direction—but meeting places and a headquarters were fast becoming necessary to preserve the fruit of the revival.

Early in May, a parcel of ground was purchased in what was known as the Horse Fair in Bristol. A room, large enough to accommodate two of the societies, was erected at once, and the foundation stone of the first Methodist meeting place was laid.

John, in order to keep control of the mushrooming community of born-again believers, took the whole financial responsibility upon himself. He had no funds with which to work, but he contended that he knew the earth was the Lord's and the fullness thereof. In the first few days of the adventure, he incurred a liability of more than a hundred and fifty pounds, which was only a beginning.

As the building took shape, two burdens lay heavily on the narrow shoulders of John Wesley. The first and most important was the old problem of nurturing the converts—keeping them growing in grace and knowledge. The other: how to underwrite the expanding financial need.

When the demand for funds became acute, John called together the leading men in the project and presented the problem. One of these was a strong, levelheaded layman known as Captain Foy.

"We have an asset in numbers," Foy explained. "Let everyone give a penny a week, and the money will be raised."

"But our people are poor," said another. "Many of them cannot afford to do it. They can barely keep bread on their tables."

"That is so," agreed the captain. "Let us divide the people into groups of twelve, each with a leader. Put eleven of the poorest with me. I will call upon them once a week. For those who cannot afford to share, I will give for them as well as for myself. If enough others are willing to do the same, our problem will be solved."

The plan worked well, eventually lifting both of Wesley's burdens. The leaders, relating the progress of their groups, reported laxness in the way many of the Christians were beginning to live. They called it backsliding.

"Good!" cried John. "This is exactly what I have been praying for!"

The men looked at Wesley in amazement, wondering if the load he had been carrying had become too heavy.

"Not the backsliding," he explained. "The remedy! You have stumbled onto it. We shall divide all the people into classes and appoint leaders of good report. They will inquire into the spiritual progress of their charges every week."

Thus it was that the class meeting, the hallmark of the Methodist movement, was born that day in Bristol.

Persecution soon began to show its ugly face. The transformed lives of the converts were fast becoming an embarrassment to nominal Christians. And the enthusiasm displayed in public meetings became more and more offensive, especially to those outside the inner circle of believers.

Early in June, John met this new problem head-on in a meeting at Bath—a playground for the wealthy and a city steeped in sin. A prominent townsman by the name of Beau Nash had received exaggerated reports of enthusiasm exhibited in Wesley's out-of-door services. Nash was an overbearing, self-appointed czar in all civic affairs. He bragged that he would put a stop to the next meeting John Wesley should try to conduct in this ancient city with its constant flow of visitors from far and near.

As a result of the boasting, nearly the whole city of Bath was present the next time John prepared to preach. The rich and famous from Dublin, London, Paris, and beyond gathered in to see the fun. But the fun quickly gave way to an unexpected seriousness as John proceeded to show that the Scriptures teach that all are under sin. Then Nash, elbowing his way through the mass, confronted the preacher.

"By what authority do you do these things?" he bellowed.

"By authority of Jesus Christ," John answered. "It was conveyed to me when the (now) archbishop of Canterbury laid hands on me and said, 'Take thou authority to preach the Gospel.'"

"This meeting is a conventicle!" Nash fairly screamed. "As such, it is contrary to an Act of Parliament."

"Wrong," spoke Wesley quietly. "There is nothing seditious about this gathering, hence it is not a conventicle."

"I say it is," the angry man roared. "And besides, your preaching scares the wits out of people!"

"Sir," said John. "Did you ever hear me preach before?"

"No," Nash answered.

"How, then, can you judge by what you have never heard?" asked Wesley.

"By common report," said Nash, who was beginning to weaken.

"That is not enough," John retorted. "Give me leave, sir, to ask whether your name is Nash?"

"My name is Nash!" the man fairly screamed.

"I dare not judge you by common report," said John. "It is not enough to judge by."

Baffled, Nash took a minute to recover. "I desire to know what these people come here for," he cried.

Suddenly, a portly woman stepped into the picture. "Sir," she said addressing Wesley. "You leave him to me. Let an old woman answer him!" Then, turning to Nash and shaking a stubby finger in his face, barely missing the tip of his long, narrow nose, she said between clenched teeth, "You, Mr. Nash, take care of your body. We take care of our souls. Food for our souls is why we come here!"

Nash, clearly beaten at his own game, slunk away.

A battle had been won, but John was certain that far more drastic persecution than that was smoldering, waiting to burst into flame. For the first time, though, he felt secure in the thought that the revival was on a footing strong enough to either save or repel its enemies.

John received a letter in the post that disturbed him greatly. Troubles were threatening the very life of the Fetter Lane Society in London. "Please come home as soon as possible" was the earnest plea. He gave last-minute orders to his leaders. Paramount in his instruction was the necessity of keeping the class meetings alive and well.

"They will have to take the place of preaching services

until I or some other ordained man of the faith can be secured to serve the pulpits," he explained. (At that point in Wesley's thinking, a man without proper credentials had no right to preach the glorious gospel of Christ.)

Before the week was over, John was back in London. Whitefield and Charles were overjoyed. Problems too difficult for them to handle were about to destroy the strongest society of believers in the city. A spirit of mysticism, sponsored by a different kind of Moravian than Peter Bohler, was splitting the loosely knit organism down the middle. John was able to temporarily stem the tide, but he was aware that a London headquarters, not unlike the one he was establishing in Bristol, was fast becoming necessary to preserve the fruit of the revival there.

Whitefield was preaching to vast crowds in the great out-of-doors in London and its environs. Charles, not yet convinced that out-of-door preaching was "decent and in order," demanded a roof be over his head while he was "rightly dividing the word of truth." Both men were successful in their own way. The revival was rolling. Finally, John and George succeeded in convincing Charles that Jesus, preaching from Peter's boat, surely enjoyed the approval of heaven.

That year was one of marvelous transition for the Wesleys. The revival was working wonders—first within the family and hence, through their witness, in thousands of souls.

Susanna always had been one of the world's best women in her own right, rigidly keeping the commandments of God. No one who knew her ever denied that. But after "a legal night of seventy years,"* while taking

---

* These words were taken from Susanna's epitaph, which was written by her son Charles.

the cup at Communion, the words of the ritual struck through to her heart and she knew that God for Christ's sake had forgiven her all her sins. Such was her "eleventh hour" confession to son John.

In the autumn of 1739, Sammy Wesley, who walked as straight as an arrow, was taken suddenly ill at the age of forty-nine, but not until after he was convinced that miracles of God attended the awakening he opposed so sternly. While Sammy never openly identified himself with the revival, one who attended him through the long hours of his illness said: "God gave him a calm and full assurance of his interest in Christ." Sammy died in peace. John, whose differences with this elder brother had been fully reconciled, spoke with passion: "Oh, may everyone who opposes the revival be thus convinced that this doctrine is of God."

Later that autumn, John purchased a tract of land near Bunnhill Fields, outside the city, upon which stood the ruins of an old foundry. With the help of many hands who longed for a permanent place of worship, the dilapidated building was transformed into a chapel and a living quarters for those who would labor there for souls. Susanna was among the first to take residence at the foundry. And it was she who convinced her two remaining sons that their High Church prejudices only hindered the revival that God had entrusted to their care. John—acting reluctantly at first upon her excellent advice—appointed twenty lay preachers to take to the fields and preach the gospel to every creature.

CHAPTER XI

Controversy

John Wesley, who had returned to London from Bristol to help settle a Fetter Lane Society dispute, succeeded only in retarding its progress. It became evident that division in the shape of a triangle was about to destroy this excellent fellowship of believers.

The trouble began when a Moravian minister, Pastor Molther, assumed leadership of the Fetter Lane Society. Following the steps of Peter Bohler, this man, heading for Pennsylvania, stopped over in London to enhance his grasp of the English tongue and was then detracted into staying and leading the society. He was tall, handsome, and strong, with a magnetic personality hard to resist. He possessed every quality needed to direct and promote spiritual life in the society. However, an element in his theology known as "stillness," in which sinners were exhorted to do nothing but wait for the Lord to call them, put him at odds with most of the brethern.

The Moravians, an introverted society, would have

had little adverse influence on the revival except that a second side of the disturbing triangle projected itself at the same time. Whitefield, whose background was unlike that of John and Charles, was beginning to preach the doctrine of election to salvation and reprobation.

Diametrically opposed to election, the Wesleys provided the third side of the triangle, preaching free grace in conversion and holiness of heart—a separate experience available to all born-again Christians.

Now that the disruptive triangle was complete, the magnificent awakening, begun by Whitefield and carried on by the Wesleys, was in serious trouble.

In a quiet corner of a pleasant tea garden, Benjamin Ingham and Charles Delamotte sat once again engaged in earnest conversation. The Fetter Lane affair was particularly disturbing to these young men who had been so deeply entrenched in Wesley's earlier theory of salvation by works alone. Both men by this time had accepted Christ as their personal Savior.

Where do we go from here? was their unanswered query. Ever since their student days at Oxford, when the Holy Club was molding their lives, they had diligently kept the ordinances of God. Hence, to live a carefully disciplined life was hardly a cross to bear for either of these two fellows. If there had been only one evangelical path to pursue, they might have skipped along, singing, praising the Lord. But their three friends—Molther, Whitefield, and Wesley—were each dogmatically defending what seemed to be widely different interpretations of the Word.

"One of them must be right," Ingham reasoned carefully. "That means two of them must be wrong."

Delamotte's response was interrupted by the approach of a handsome, cheerful young fellow with a broad smile, whom both men recalled from Oxford days as Wilson Beck. Wilson was the type of fellow everyone remembers. He had introduced Dan Dunlevy, the lecturer, the night the Wesley brothers and Peter Bohler had gone to hear the message "Why Kingdoms Fall."

In describing Wilson to Susanna and his sister Kezzie, Charles Wesley once said, "He is the kind of person who gives the impression that he never forgets a name or a face. And while he often makes a nuisance of himself with his constant flow of compliments, agreeing with everyone and everything, he hasn't an enemy in the world. He is one of the most brilliant fellows I've ever met. Even so, he appears to make little practical use of his wealth of knowledge. He never actually enrolled at the university—that would have been a boring experience for him. But he was forever getting permission to sit in on lectures of special interest and reading good books incessantly. Wilson lives with a wealthy uncle for whom he works, keeping his accounts."

This confirmed individualist entered the tea garden. The two friends stood to greet him.

"Well now," Wilson cried joyfully, "Delamotte and Ingham, two of my best friends of the good old days. I see you are involved in serious discussion, but I hope you have time to tell me about yourselves."

"Yes," said Ingham. "Sit down. Maybe you can help us with a problem."

After a few moments of good-natured banter, the three men, sitting at the tiny tea table, discussed the subject at hand. Ingham introduced the three-way theological conflict that was threatening the future existence of the Fetter Lane Society. Serious questions, he said, were being raised in the minds of many members, including Delamotte and himself.

Wilson smiled broadly. "You see three roads ahead, only one of which you assume will lead you to heaven. Am I right?"

"Something like that," said Delamotte.

"My good friend Dan Dunlevy and I discussed this very subject at length in our study of the revival he foresaw as England's only salvation. Dan died recently, only several days after he made his own eternal peace with God." Wilson paused in a futile effort to control his emotions. "He and I passed that milestone together," he added, quickly regaining his composure. "We both knew the teaching long before we knew the Christ."

"We heard about Dunlevy's passing," said Ingham soberly. "We're sorry. But we are certainly happy to hear that both you and he were converted. We will want to hear more about that."

"I can see you fellows are both doing well," said Wilson, hitting his old stride again. "You'll be mightily used of God if you take the right road."

Ingham studied the speaker's face closely. He sensed something akin to the proverbial tongue-in-cheek remark in his complimentary statement.

Wilson read Ingham's thoughts, too. "I'm sorry," he said. "You'll discover soon that I am as serious as any child of God can be. Let us begin with the bright side—the promise that God has provided a way into the kingdom through the shed blood of Christ. This, the Bible clearly states, is available only by grace through faith. I'm sure the three leaders in the division will agree with this."

"They will," said Delamotte. "The three roads branch out from there."

"Well," said Wilson. "We need to get a look into the heart of the problem. Will one of you fellows give a quick survey of the three systems that have you so deeply disturbed?"

"Ingham, you're a man of few words," said Delamotte. "I will gladly yield the floor to you."

"All right," Ingham responded. "I'll try.

"The Wesleys," he began, "contend that a fullness of the Spirit—a heart cleansing—is available in this life subsequent to regeneration. In search of that experience, John's admonition to believers is simple: 'Seek nothing but more love.' He claims that growth in grace and knowledge come more easily and quickly following heart cleansing. He contends further that a believer is still a creature of choice, capable of rejecting the Christ he once accepted.

"If that describes the Wesleys, I'll move on to Molther's case," Ingham exclaimed.

"You've done exceptionally well," said Wilson, flashing his most appreciative smile. "Go on, by all means."

Ingham hesitated momentarily, collecting his thoughts.

"Molther," he continued, "teaches that no one has any degree of faith until he enjoys this full assurance of grace. Forgiveness and cleansing, he infers, must necessarily be received simultaneously. This experience may be entered into only through what he calls *stillness*. 'Be still and know that I am God.' He tells sinners to give up the public means of grace. Bible study, praying, and good works are of no value at this point. Sinners will come to know God intuitively through this contemplative stillness. Growth in grace begins with one's acceptance of Christ.

"Delamotte," Ingham asked, "do you have anything to add to what I'm trying to say?"

"No," Delamotte answered slowly. "If Wilson is satisfied with your description, I surely am."

"No one could tell it better," said Wilson. "Now, what about Whitefield?"

"George Whitefield holds to the doctrine of predestination. According to the teaching—as I understand it—everyone's relationship with a sovereign God has been determined back somewhere in the eons of eternity. Hence, only the elect are saved, and they cannot be lost." Ingham paused. "I'll have to admit," he said, "that I am ill-prepared to speak intelligently regarding this theology. I have been so closely associated with the Wesleys and the Moravians that I have never taken time to study it.

"I do know that George Whitefield is one of the best evangelists of the day," he continued. "Hundreds of sinners get soundly converted under his preaching. I have great faith in him."

"Thank you, Ingham," said Delamotte warmly. "It would have taken me an hour to do what you have done in minutes."

"Amazing," said Wilson. "Don't you suppose that eventually these men will find it pleasing to the Lord to make some adjustments in their philosophies? At least to file away the sharp edges?"

"I hope so," said Delamotte seriously. "John Wesley argues that the stern position Whitefield is taking is absurd. It makes God the creator of souls who have no hope of redemption. I have to agree, but my mother needed the sense of security Whitefield's preaching promised. Father agrees with Wesley, but for the sake of unity in the home, he makes no issue of it."

Wilson stood to his feet, caught the eye of the one

available waiter, and ordered tea and crumpets for three. Then, for several minutes, resting his hands on the back of the chair before him, he spoke his deepest thoughts.

"These are good men we've been discussing," he said. "I assume they agree that, following conversion, it becomes a Christian's duty to obey the Lord and grow in grace and knowledge."

"Exactly," Ingham answered.

"In light of this," Wilson continued thoughtfully, "doesn't it seem that these leaders should find common ground for fellowship and ministry the remainder of the way?"

"Of course," agreed Delamotte, "but not one of them is about to concede that he is wrong."

"Should one," asked Wilson, "since each believes he has the mind of God?"

"We don't have an answer to that," Ingham answered honestly. "If you were asked to debate the issue with any one of the men, how would you go about it?"

"I wouldn't," responded Wilson promptly, flashing his most engaging smile. "I would ask him kindly to explain his position, documenting it with the plain Word of God. And any one of the three would do that rather well, I'm sure. Then I would congratulate him honestly, saying that many sinners will find salvation, peace, comfort, a sense of security, and will grow in grace and knowledge by pursuing the way he leads."

Wilson resumed his seat, ate his crumpet, and sipped his tea. Then he continued earnestly: "I would be inferring that many other Christians, owing to different backgrounds, personalities, and needs, might find little or no comfort in his interpretation of truth. Hence, he should be neither offended nor grieved when some believers follow the steps of another."

"I'm beginning to understand you," said Delamotte thoughtfully. "It grieves both Ingham and me to see John Wesley and George Whitefield—two of the best friends we have in the world—disagreeing over a theological position to the point of breaking fellowship."

Wilson smiled again. "Don't worry," he said. "The Lord saw through all this long before we had a chance to look at it. It simply fit into His plan. God knows that both men are honest, dedicated, and sincere—serving Him with all diligence. Someday, they will be good friends working together again. Both men will make concessions, but we shouldn't expect either of them to cast away his convictions. Each will condone the other, meeting in fellowship at the foot of the cross. Then they will work together in the revival, allowing their converts to choose the course of their preference. I believe this because I have faith in God. 'He is not willing that any should perish.' I also have faith in Wesley and Whitefield. Lesser men will carry the fight to their graves, each consigning the other and all his followers to the pit. They are the ones that Satan will use."

"One thing bothers me, Wilson," said Ingham thoughtfully. "Are we to understand you are completely neutral in matters such as these?"

"Oh no," Wilson answered quickly. "One system seems more logical and certainly more helpful to me, personally, than any other. Dan Dunlevy and I considered this at length. Fortunately, we were not of the same mind in this, which gave us opportunity to be objective in our study. We made a covenant with God and kept it until Dan died. Now I continue it alone. Every morning in my private devotions, I say: 'Dear Lord, I thank you for your Word that gives me peace of mind and a sense of security in you. Today, I will do my best to serve you—to grow in grace and knowledge. Help me to be tolerant of those whose needs are different than mine—to have Christian fellowship with all Thy children. Amen.'"

Benjamin Ingham and Charles Delamotte found themselves on the horns of a dilemma. Their friendship with John and Charles Wesley was of long standing, without a blemish. To align themselves with John Wesley in the current controversy seemed as natural as life.

On the other hand, they had always enjoyed excellent rapport with George Whitefield. He had been a friend indeed and a friend in need. To join with him would have certain advantages. Whitefield was planning another trip to America. Ingham and Delamotte wanted to return to Georgia. Joining with Whitefield would provide them an opportunity.

The problems they faced were old ones. To cast their lots with either man would be an affront to the other. Maintaining the friendship of both the Wesleys and Whitefield was most important. Also, a decision in favor of one or the other would tend to position the two young men theologically. They were not ready for this. Nothing in their background of training and experience led them toward Whitefield and the stern tenets of predestination and election. And Wesley's contention that a second climactic experience awaited the regenerated heart was not easy for these men to abide.

They had sought holiness of heart through the nearly impossible rules of the Holy Club long before they even heard of salvation by faith. When they were finally born again, they felt they had already accomplished through self-discipline everything needed for heart cleansing. "What more can we do?" they asked.

One way out remained. They could join the Moravians. Both Ingham and Delamotte had come to appreciate these devout Germans on board the good ship *Simmonds*. They had worked closely with them in Savannah. With the exception of the Wesleys and Whitefield, no one in their experience equaled Peter Bohler in godliness and good sense. He had led John and Charles Wesley to the foot of the cross. Pastor Molther had fascinated both Ingham and Delamotte with his winsome, personal charm. The Moravian work in the colonies was growing steadily which would eventually open the way for these two young missionaries to return to Georgia. And theologically, surely Ingham and Delamotte fit the Moravian pattern—right or wrong—of full salvation received simultaneously with regeneration.

Their best friends, the Wesleys and Whitefield, could have given them a long string of reasons why they ought not to identify themselves with this sectarian society. But no opportunity was afforded. Ingham and Delamotte joined the Moravians. Wesley Hall, James Hutton, and others of the Holy Club joined the German society, too. However, they did not endorse Molther's doctrine of stillness.

The controversy between the Wesleys and Whitefield became more and more intense. And their followers soon became so adamant and vociferous in the growing debate that the leaders were forced to rebuke them.

Wilson Beck walked quietly, smilingly among the people of both camps—advocating tolerance and *revival* at any cost. "Continuing renewal," he claimed, "is the lifeblood of the church. As long as a spirit of renewal abides, both systems see sinners brought to Christ."

To those who listened, he asked, "Dear God, must we allow Satan to enter the arena through the finest saints on earth?"

Wilson's influence was greater probably than anyone suspected. Then he was gone. His uncle, whose interests were worldwide, sent him to India to take charge of his holdings in the ancient city of Bengal. The last missive received by a friend from Wilson Beck stated simply that he had become inadvertently involved in a political situation there in which the viceroy had been overthrown by a subordinate, Ali Verdi Khan. Beck's warm greetings to the Wesleys, Whitefield, Ingham, and Delamotte were deeply appreciated.

The extent of Wilson's influence in the eventual healing of the wounds can only be surmised, but his prophecy was valid. His faith that Whitefield and the Wesleys were "too big" to allow their prejudices to destroy the work to which they were called was finally justified. In the meantime, though, it seemed that the ugly affair would have to hit bottom before it could bounce back.

In 1740, John Wesley published a sermon entitled "Free Grace." In it, he summarized the doctrine of election, predestination, or reprobation in the following concise sentence: "The sense of all is plainly this— by virtue of an eternal, unchanging, irresistible decree of God, one part of mankind are infallibly saved, and the rest infallibly damned; it being impossible that any of the former should be damned, or any of the latter should be saved."

Wesley had made an in-depth study of free will as opposed to divine sovereignty in his student days at

Oxford fifteen years earlier. At that time, he had corresponded with his mother regarding this controversy that has been slicing away at the church, trying to divide it, since the days of Saint Augustine. John had clearly stated his position in a note to her, asking whether his logic in opposing the doctrine of predestination was sound.

She had answered in typical Susanna fashion, saying, "I firmly believe that God from eternity has elected some to eternal life; but then I humbly conceive that this election is founded on His foreknowledge, according to Romans 8:29-30. Those whom, in His eternal prescience, God saw would make a right use of their powers and accept of offered mercy, He did predestinate and adopt for His children." This expressed John's sentiments exactly.

John published his sermon, presenting precisely the view his mother had expressed in that letter years before. Charles was so deeply impressed, he wrote a lengthy hymn supporting the doctrine of free grace. One verse reads as follows:

> *Doom them an endless death to die*
> *From which they could not flee.*
> *O Lord, thine inmost bowels cry*
> *Against the dire decree!*

The publisher added Charles's poem to John's thesis.

Whitefield was in Georgia, trying to get the orphanage erected when the sermon came off the press. Two months later, a copy of it reached him in Savannah. He was greatly distressed as one would suppose. Never in his

life had he been rebuked so soundly by friend or foe as
when he read another of Charles's pointed verses:

> *And shall I, Lord, confine thy love*
> *As not to others free?*
> *And may not every sinner prove*
> *The grace that found out me?*

George Whitefield was a great soul. A lesser one
would have burned the sermon and the song, along with
all the bridges that bound him in any way to Charles and
John Wesley. Of the two, Charles was George's special
friend. Weeks later, when his emotions had returned to
normal, Whitefield wrote a friendly letter—addressed to
the brothers, but directed particularly to Charles—in
which he calmly, honestly expressed his displeasure:

> February, 1741 . . . My dear, dear brethren, why
> did you throw out the bone of contention? Why
> did you print that sermon against predestination?
> Why did you in particular, my dear brother
> Charles, affix your hymn. . . ? How can you say
> you will not dispute with me about election and still
> print such hymns, and your brother send his sermon
> over to Mr. Gardner and others in America?

Friendship ties were strained but never severed.
While, no doubt, there was a softening of lines on both
sides of the fence, the men did not cast aside their basic
beliefs. But records plainly show that the Wesleys and
Whitefield became the best of friends again and worked
together in the great revival, which was already reaching

beyond the borders of Britain. It has been said that, in this respect, they did much better than many of their followers. Particularly impressive is the knowledge that some time along the way, George Whitefield and John Wesley made a covenant that, upon the death of one, the other would bring the funeral oration.

CHAPTER XII
Trials of the Road

Far to the west of London, a blazing sun was setting as Charles Wesley gently reined his steed toward the golden horizon. Wesley's one desire was to be alone with his thoughts, where only the lowing of cattle and the song of the whippoorwill might disturb the evening silence. Charles was both poet and pastor, capable of preaching effectively to thousands in the great out-of-doors. Of this, he admitted, he was more than a little proud, but in his heart, the podium and the pulpit took second place to his prolific pen.

As he rode, he visualized a multitude of worshipers back at Moorsfield where brother John was ministering. Charles had the evening off—a rare occurrence—and he was making the most of it. His goal was Buckingham, where he could meditate undisturbed while his horse enjoyed the lush pasture.

As he traversed a narrow country lane, he spotted a circle of trees on the verdant meadow. He quickly tethered his mount where the grass was tall and inviting. Sitting upon a fallen log, he wrote as words flowed freely from heart and head and hand. Charles Wesley seldom wrote poems; he wrote poetry. Not hymns, but verses that soar from the endless fields of prose like wood nymphs dancing in circles above a quiet forest glen. Later, he would fit them together with calm deliberation just as a child who labors over a picture puzzle to produce a perfect image. Of course, Charles could not imagine his lines would be sung by millions of worshipers in churches of many creeds throughout centuries yet unborn.

He wrote as inspiration blessed his troubled soul:

> *The blessing of thy love bestow;*
> *For this my cries shall never fail;*
> *Wrestling, I will not let thee go,*
> *I will not, till my suit prevail.*

And again:

> *Save me from pride, the plague expel;*
> *Jesus, thine humble self impart:*
> *O let thy mind within me dwell;*
> *O give me lowliness of heart.*

Charles was in a deeply reflective mood. John was pressing him to continue a ministry fraught with nearly every peril that the apostle Paul had been forced to face. But beyond the indignities of scornful men, Charles wrestled with the decision of his continuing ministry and with whom he should associate.

Emotions were running high. Cherished, deep-abiding

friendships were about to be destroyed. Charles, in that hour of indecision, didn't think he had one inkling of what he ought to do. The difficulty between John and Whitefield was at its height. Ingham and Delamotte had joined the Moravians. Charles, too, seriously considered joining the German group. He longed for the mind of God in this, but he feared his dedication was too shallow to conform, even if he had it. The verses he had written—which later would be projected into hymns a troubled world would sing for centuries—were petitions in his own behalf. He wept as he read them over, which may be the reason those "who labor and are heavy laden" still weep as they sing them in congregations of the righteous.

Charles allowed his tears to flow. Only heaven and he were aware of their presence and potential. Then came the mind of God, for Charles Wesley was ready to receive it. Thrills of glory coursed through every fiber of his being. With great joy he reached for his pen again and wrote from a happy heart—fully consecrated to do the will of the One who called him:

> *Vilest of the sinful race,*
> *Lo! I answer to thy call.*
> *Meanest vessel of thy grace,*
> *Grace divinely free for all;*
> *Lo! I come to do thy will*
> *All thy counsel to fulfill.*

But there was more:

> *Take my soul and body's powers;*
> *Take my memory, mind and will;*

All my goods and all my hours;
All I know and all I feel;
All I think or speak or do;
Take my heart, but make it new.

Later he would add several verses to the song, but for that moment he concluded with this:

If to the right or left I stray,
That moment, Lord, reprove;
And let me weep my life away
For having grieved thy love.
O may the least omission pain
My well-instructed soul,
And drive me to the blood again
Which makes the wounded whole.

Charles began to feel that, all along, he had known the way he would have to take, but he couldn't admit it until he was ready to mind the Lord at any cost. It was settled. He would remain with John to the ends of the earth if necessary to keep the revival rolling.

Charles and John Wesley seldom traveled together. By going their separate ways, they covered twice the area and ministered to double the number of needy souls. They rode the best, well-trained horses—strong, steady geldings that needed no touch of rein or quirt to control them as they moved at steady lope in perfect rhythm. John, relaxing in the saddle with book or pad before him, read and wrote incessantly across the endless miles. Charles, too, read as he rode—mostly pages from John's religious writings—then translated the pungent truths to rhyme and song. (In 1898, a songbook published in Chicago, Illinois, would include 372 hymns by Charles Wesley. During his lifetime, he wrote twenty times as many.)

From London to Bristol to Bath, from Ireland to Scotland to Wales, the brothers rode, preaching daily to crowds estimated in multiplied thousands. Often those numbers were exaggerated by enthusiastic witnesses who had no way of counting the people. But even divided in half, they stagger the imagination.

Persecution, too, was unbelievable. Mostly it was accomplished by hungry, jobless men who were paid to destroy the Methodists. Often these ruffians had no argument with the Wesleys or the masses that gathered whenever they preached. Sometimes the mischief-makers were hired by magistrates who feared open rebellion. Angry Anglican priests paid the persecutors to go to any length to stamp out the "heretics." Homes were burned, men were flogged. Innocent women suffered the most when the godless rioters, armed with stones and clubs, knives and guns, forced their way into the houses of new-born Christians. Murder was often committed, but prosecution of the guilty was impossible under existing conditions. Scores of lay preachers, as well as the Wesleys, laid their lives on the line every time they stood to preach.

On one occasion, when John was ministering to a great out-of-doors congregation, a herd of cattle grazed peacefully in a pasture a mile away. Three horsemen rode into the herd, singled out a short-horned bull and drove him toward the assembly. As the riders approached the meeting, they began lashing the animal with their long whips until, mad with pain, the heavy beast lowered its

161

head and charged into the helpless crowd. Scores were injured, two were killed, *none were arrested.*

John stood helpless in his improvised pulpit as the people scattered. He watched a poor widow and the child of a recently converted couple being fatally gored by the horns of an angry bull. Finally, brave men succeeded in driving the distracted animal away.

For an hour, John ministered to the wounded and bereaved. To the shocked and suffering who watched him go about his priestly duty, John was an emissary from heaven. They didn't know that the wiry little preacher was quietly, secretly contemplating an admission of defeat. Satan was within an inch of stamping out one of the greatest threats in centuries to his evil kingdom.

Persecution was no stranger to John Wesley. He had suffered threats and thrashings, often escaping barely with his life. All such he had taken with amazing grace, but this brutal, wanton attack upon innocent, defenseless worshipers in his congregation was nigh a crushing blow.

When Wesley's great temptation became known to a number of his friends, they implored him to press on—all to no avail. John shut himself away in the home of a friend and sent a courier to Charles who was ministering in Bristol, thirty miles away. John's missive was received with great alarm. Between the lines, Charles read a message of complete abandon. He saddled his mount and rode through the night to his brother's side. There, through the morning hours, they talked and wept and tried to pray.

"I feel like a murderer," John cried in desperation, as Charles struggled in vain to pacify his brother's tortured mind. Then, a quiet rap on the door startled the men to attention. Answering the summons, John stood facing the mayor of the town, Major White, an avowed enemy of the Methodists.

"May I come in?" the mayor asked.

"Of course," said John sadly. "I have neither strength nor desire to present a defense of the tragedy I'm sure you have come to discuss. I have just told my brother Charles that I am about to concede defeat for, while I am ready to die a martyr, I can no longer be an instrument in the senseless destruction of innocent human life."

"Well, now," the mayor began as he took John's extended hand. "Perhaps my little visit is providential. I consider myself a Christian—an active communicant in the Church of England and a loyal subject of the Crown. It is true that I have opposed the Methodists because I feared an insurrection of the masses. But recently I have had a change of mind, if hardly what you people call a change of heart."

"Thank you," said Charles, smiling broadly. (John was speechless.) "Please be seated. Allow me to say that this preamble to whatever you have come to deliver is hardly what my brother and I anticipated."

"I'm sure it isn't," the dignified gentleman answered as he took the proffered chair. "I have not been blind to the rising moral standards of our populace in the wake of the movement you men have launched in our beloved but near-apostate Commonwealth. I am aware, of course, that you have been refused permission to conduct out-of-door meetings on our village green. After the despicable conduct of ruffians that resulted in two deaths and many serious injuries just outside my jurisdiction yesterday, I am here to give you men a standing invitation to conduct services on the common with the best police protection we can provide. I ask only that you do whatever you can to curb the enthusiasm in the meetings that is responsible for nearly all the criticism we receive concerning the conduct of your followers."

John regained his composure in time to answer the unexpected speech. "We are grateful indeed," he said, "for your kind support and generous offer. You have cured my ills. May I respond briefly to two points of special import that you have made?"

"Of course, of course," the mayor spoke heartily, leaning forward to show his interest.

"First," said John, "my brother and I do not deserve the credit you accord us in initiating the revival that is sweeping Britain. George Whitefield—a greater preacher than either Charles or I—first dared break with tradition and present the gospel beyond the walls of churches to crowds that reached into the thousands. Mr. Whitefield is in America now, enjoying similar success. At his request we took leadership of the movement here.

"Second," John continued, "we have been unable to control the enthusiasm of which you speak. We are often embarrassed by it. Certainly we have never done anything to promote or intentionally stimulate it. While we cannot speak for all the men employed in the field, our instruction to them has been to follow our example as nearly as they can."

"Please continue," the mayor answered. "I will need this information in answering my own critics when you accept my invitation to bring your meetings into town."

"Just one thing more," said John. "We sometimes see hardened sinners fall as dead while we are preaching, then later, arise converted. Freed from their sinful habits and wicked attitudes, they become a part of that rising moral standard of which you spoke only moments ago. Some people say such demonstration is of the devil, but we counter with the question, 'When and why has Satan started making good men out of bad ones?'

"An explanation of this phenomenon in part," continued John, "may be that many of these men and women are poor, untutored souls, whose habit has been to allow full freedom of their emotions. As more and more sophisticated people join us, we should see this reaction to the intervention of God receding. But since God is working wonders, forgive us if we do not feel free to interfere."

That day, June 27, 1742, was a great day in the lives of the Wesleys. The tables began to turn in favor of the awakening, but years would be involved in its full acceptance.

Charles, as deeply moved as was his brother by this turn, wrote:

> *Strive we, in affection strive;*
> *Let the purer flame revive;*
> *Such as in the martyrs glowed,*
> *Dying champions for their God:*
> *We like them may live and love;*
> *Called we are their joys to prove;*
> *Saved with them from future wrath;*
> *Partners of like precious faith.*

John was fully restored to his normal mental health by the visit of the mayor. But through the troubling experience, both John and Charles saw the danger of breaking beneath the awful strain of their labors. Before Charles returned to his field, the two brothers agreed to meet periodically for the single purpose of sharing their problems—unburdening their souls. Three times during the year that followed they did exactly that.

John and Charles Wesley were wonderfully blessed with two important elements in their natures. One was a courageous faith supported by a lifetime of disciplined training; the other, a healthy sense of humor. We hear little of the latter, but it must not be ignored. Unlike their mother in this respect, the sons of Susanna allowed themselves to laugh. During the tense days of severe persecution, when they met to unburden their hearts and praise the Lord for His miraculous hand, they made it a point to laugh at the humorous side of their nigh-hopeless situations.

In 1742, the brothers spent a day together in their old hometown of Epworth for just such a time of relaxation. They walked the familiar streets together, passing the parsonage where they had sat at the feet of their meticulous mother. They talked of pleasant evenings when they danced with their sisters and played games with their parents and the girls. Charles wanted to go in—to satisfy a nostalgic longing—but John remarked that they would not be welcome.

"Why not?" asked Charles. "Surely the rector or his lady will understand our interest and allow us to see inside the house again."

Nothing more was said as they walked on across the open glebe toward the quaint but grand old church where their father had served as rector for nearly forty long, difficult years. John pointed to his father's gravestone—a large, flat, oblong block of granite that stood beside the ancient building.

"Father would be honored to have us sit together on his monument to discuss the revival he long predicted," said John. "Let us do that, and I will tell you why I fear the rector would not welcome us to his home." When they were seated, John continued. "I came here less than two weeks ago, Charles, hoping to preach from our father's pulpit."

"Go on," said the brother. "I can guess the rest but I want to hear it."

"Early Sunday morning," said John, "I knocked at the door of the parish house and was met by the rector who showed little interest in my presence. He must have been preparing early for his office for the smell of liquor was plainly on his breath. I offered to assist him, either with the elements or in the pulpit, but he declined. 'Your reputation arrived here ahead of you,' he stated with a smirk. 'Not one person would remain for the sacrament if you were allowed to perform a priestly duty,' the rector snarled.

"I smiled," said John, "and asked him to forgive me. I told him as kindly as possible that I would never knowingly be an instrument in the hands of Satan."

The brothers arose and made their way to the church door. "No one can deny us the privilege of entering the sanctuary for the purpose of prayer," said John. They entered the empty building and knelt in a prolonged season of intercession for the hungry masses around them in Lincolnshire. Then they went outside and sat together beneath a shady tree they remembered well.

"Did you attend the Sunday worship?" Charles inquired.

"Of course," John answered. "You may guess toward whom the sermon was directed. The rector took for his text 'Quench not the Spirit' and pointed out that exercising enthusiasm was a most dangerous way of breaking this commandment. Then the otherwise dignified minister turned actor," John explained. "He mimicked with talent, I must admit, the oratorical manner of many of our lay ministers. I'm sure everyone got the message. At the door I tried to congratulate him on his representation of a Methodist preacher, suggesting that someday he might make a good one himself." John smiled at the thought of his own audacity.

Charles laughed. "How did he respond to that?" he asked.

"He ignored me completely," John answered. "Really, I can't blame him. He faced a problem in that a number of his parishioners were listening—among them, our friend John Taylor. Outside, Taylor asked me whether I would preach in the churchyard at six o'clock that evening. I told him I would, of course. Then he spread the word around."

"I'm sure you had a crowd," said Charles, who was thoroughly enjoying the picture John was presenting.

"I did indeed," John answered seriously. "When the appointed time arrived, the largest congregation Epworth ever witnessed assembled on the green. I stood on Father's tombstone and preached from the text 'The kingdom of God is not meat and drink; but righteousness, and peace, and joy in the Holy Ghost.' The response was excellent. The people begged me to remain and preach again the following evening. I did, and every evening throughout the week."

"Is that the end?" asked Charles.

"No," answered John, smiling again in anticipation of fixing a humorous climax to the story. "Each morning and afternoon I preached in neighboring communities. During the week, I visited a justice of the peace in Wroot who was said to have shown a candor and good feeling that are rare enough in these days. The good man welcomed me with a hug, asking whether a story about some of my critics might lift my spirits. I told him I was certain that such an account would be most helpful.

"'Well, sir,' the justice began, 'yesterday a wagonload of your new converts were brought before me by angry neighbors who haven't yet seen the light. When I asked what these people had done, a long silence followed. No one seemed to think that the matter would be questioned. Finally, an old fellow spoke up and said that these heretics pray from morning till night and think they are better than anybody.'"

Charles smiled. "I guess he could hardly bring charges against them for that," he said.

"No," John answered. "The justice asked them if they had anything more to bring before him. The old accuser said, 'Yes sir, I have. An't please yer worship, they have *converted* my wife. Till she went among them, she had such a tongue! Now she is quiet as a lamb.'"

John fought to control his mirth. "The justice told me that he looked fiercely at the old fellow and said, 'Carry them back! Carry them back, and let them convert all the scolds in town.'"

For several weeks, John and Charles Wesley had been preaching in the hardest of places, facing alone the most impossible situations. There had been nothing to relieve the strain; their most earnest petitions for peace had apparently gone unanswered. This day's laughter was just the therapy the Wesleys needed. A bit of harmless humor became an unexpected answer to their most fervent prayers. Their minds and hearts were cleared.

"There is more to tell," said John. "The best is yet to come. Our widowed brother-in-law, John Whitelamb, is still rector at Wooten, as you know. He mourns our sister's early death, still blaming himself, for he says he should have known Mary's twisted body could not bring forth a child.

"The final Sunday of my visit, he implored me to preach from his pulpit without regard for the hierarchy, which might well demand his dismissal. I arose early and quickly made the five-mile trip. The church was packed to overflowing with many seekers from afar, straining to hear the gospel through every open window and the gaping doors. Twice that afternoon I preached again. Then, back at Epworth for a final service, preaching from Father's tomb, I faced the greatest multitude of all. The people came from all directions. How I wish our father and mother could have been standing by my side."

The brothers sat in silence, musing for many minutes. Then John spoke again. "Oh, let none think his labor of love is lost because the fruit does not immediately appear," he barely whispered. "Nearly forty years, our father labored here with little fruit for his efforts. I took some pains among this people, too, and spent my strength in vain. But now the fruit appears."

"Where do you go from here?" asked Charles.

"Back home to the foundry," answered John. "Mother is failing fast. I want to tell her of the victories at Epworth and Wroot. I hope you can get home soon, my brother. Time is running out for the dearest friend we ever had."

A warm afternoon in July, John reined his steed before the foundry and hurried in to see his mother. His sister Kezzie, fighting tears, took his hand and led him to Susanna's room. Serenely quiet, the mother of the Wesleys lay dying, but at the sound of John's voice, her strength momentarily returned.

Susanna and John enjoyed one last precious meeting

of minds and hearts as he told her of the mighty crowds that packed the Epworth churchyard to hear him preach from his father's tomb.

"You will remember," he said, "that for many years, Father predicted a great revival. Mother," John continued softly, "a great awakening has come to England. Surely God is allowing Father to see it from the vantage point of heaven." Looking down into her lovely eyes, he saw a flicker of response far more revealing than tongue and lips could possibly convey. Then, calling upon the last of her waning strength, she asked that her daughters join him at her side.

"Please, my children," she said, "as soon as I am released, sing a psalm of praise to God."

From that moment she lay sheltered in an undisturbed and peaceful rest. Two days later—a few hours before the younger son arrived to greet her—Susanna quietly breathed her last. The day was July 27, 1742. She had reached the age of seventy-three. Her two remaining sons were forty and thirty-six.

When Charles arrived, he stood sadly looking down upon the lovely countenance that had never lost its beauty or its charm. The world's greatest writer of sacred stanza brushed away a tear and said, "I'm sorry, Mother. I wanted to talk with you again, but an angel has already penned your name in heaven. There, in the Lamb's Book of Life, it remains forever."

Charles left the room to put his thoughts on paper, lest they be forever lost. At his brother's desk, he wrote:

> *Meet for the fellowship above,*
> *She heard the call, "Arise my love!"*

"I come," her dying looks replied,
And lamb-like, as her Lord, she died.

Later, at the request of John and his sisters, Charles wrote a four-verse epitaph for her gravestone concluding with those inspired lines.

CHAPTER XIII

Work, Wedlock, and Song

Susanna Wesley was laid to rest in Bunnhill Fields not far
from the foundry on August 1, 1742. During her last
days, nothing would have pleased her more than to have
been told that she could be buried beside her husband at
Epworth, where they had spent thirty-nine long, hard
years together. But she had understood that to transport
a body over two hundred miles of rough terrain and
little-used trails would be practically impossible. The
lovely cemetery at Bunnhill Fields, now a part of London, was the next best choice. Buried there were many
old friends and relatives, including her favorite sister,
Elizabeth. John Bunyan, Daniel Defoe, and other important persons outside the established church were in-
terred there, too—those whose names would live for
centuries in the hearts of the people. Susanna could not
have known that her own name would be remembered
and revered by millions of Methodists and other lovers
of God through ages unknown. She did know that,

through her sons, a revival was rolling across the isles of Britain and beyond. What more could she have asked?

Soon after the funeral, John and Charles rode sadly away to their labors of love. Month after month, year after year, they pursued their arduous schedules. Persecutors continued to harass their followers as well as themselves.

A warm spring day greeted the city of Wednesbury in 1744. Birds were singing and children were playing out-of-doors after a long, wet winter. Womenfolk raked their gardens while their husbands labored in the mines. Several hundred souls had been saved in a revival that swept the area, and they proudly called themselves Methodists. Others, sneering, called them that, too. A Mrs. Sitch, not feeling well, remained in bed that day. Waking in midmorning, she prayed a prayer of thanks for herself and her neighbors who, up to then, had been spared the horrible harassment suffered by many of their friends.

"But if it comes, dear God," she said, "give us grace and strength to endure it, for we love Thee more than life."

Then it came! A rock crashed through the window, smashing the pane to pieces. The startled woman heard the front door burst asunder, admitting five rough men armed with axes and snarls of hatred. Tables and cupboards were slashed to ruin. Mrs. Sitch hid her face in her pillow and prayed, hoping the men would leave her alone upon finding her ill. But alas, they showed no mercy. She was grabbed by the arm and dragged to the floor as swinging axes smashed the bed to bits and musty feathers filled the air. The devastation to her home could hardly have been worse. In the same way, the homes of hundreds of innocent Christians were destroyed.

Charles, who faced an unfortunate fracas at Walsall,

wrote: "The mobsters roared, shouted, and threw stones incessantly. Many struck without hurting me." He went on preaching, signifying no thought of retaliation. Then two stones hit him in the face. Pausing long enough to wipe away the blood, he finished his sermon and asked the people to bow their heads in prayer. A severely agitated officer elbowed his way through the crowd to confront the praying preacher. With a dramatic gesture, the soldier drew his sword. Charles paused in his prayer to unbutton his waistcoat and shirt, exposing his broad, firm breast to the point of the weapon.

"I fear God," he said calmly, "and I honor the king."

The officer studied him for a moment, then quietly put up his sword and walked away. A lively discussion ensued. Some said that the soldier, recognizing bravery when he saw it, withdrew in genuine respect for valor. The Christians said it was God. Charles simply buttoned up his garments and continued his prayer.

By autumn 1745 the evangelists could have relaxed a bit if consciences would have allowed it, for the revival was progressing under its own power. In addition to their heavy preaching loads, the brothers were busy appointing lay leaders, instructing them in approved methods of conducting class meetings, visiting the sick, and providing for the needy. Those leaders, in turn, were teaching the members under their care to be effective witnesses for Christ.

This work, however, was not as hard and time-consuming as the preparation of helpers—converts feeling the call of God to preach. To "rightly divide the word of truth" in manner, speech, and dignity—with discipline becoming to a minister of Jesus Christ—was a sacred trust the Wesleys demanded of every preacher. The following twelve rules that John prepared for the helpers are still cherished as guiding principles for evangelical ministers of various faiths.

1. Be diligent. Never be triflingly employed. Never *while* away time nor spend more time at any place than is strictly necessary.
2. Be serious. Let your motto be Holiness to the Lord. Avoid all lightness, jesting, and foolish talking.
3. Converse sparingly and cautiously with women, particularly with young women.
4. Take no step toward marriage without solemn prayer to God and consulting with your brethren.
5. Believe evil of no one unless fully proved; take heed how you credit it. Put the best construction you can on everything. You know the judge is supposed to be on the prisoner's side.
6. Speak evil of no one, else *your* word, especially, would eat as doth a canker; keep your thoughts within your own breast till you come to the person concerned.
7. Tell everyone what you think wrong in him, lovingly and plainly, and as soon as may be, else it will fester in your own heart. Make all haste to cast the fire out of your bosom.
8. Do not effect the gentleman (appear to be of high degree). A preacher of the Gospel is the servant of all.
9. Be ashamed of nothing but sin; no, not of cleaning your own shoes when necessary.
10. Be punctual. Do everything exactly at the

time. And do not amend our rules, but keep
them, and that for conscience's sake.

11. You have nothing to do but to save souls.
Therefore spend and be spent in this work.
And go always, not only to those who want
you, but to those who want you most.

12. Act in all things, not according to your own
will, but as a son in the Gospel. . . . Therefore,
you will need all the grace and sense you have,
and to have all your wits about you. . . .

The Methodist ministry was not an easy road to travel.

Annual conferences added much in establishing Methodist foundations on a sound and practical basis. A strong
fellowship developed between the preachers, and a spirit
of unity prevailed. The worst of the persecution eventually passed and the Methodist movement no longer was
limited primarily to the poor and oppressed. Affluent,
cultured families were beginning to take their places beside what once were called "the despised few." Their
presence tended to temper the enthusiasm in the meetings.

As the persecutors withdrew, counterfeiters appeared.
Upon being apprehended, these men, drawing crowds
for the purpose of personal gain, cast suspicion upon all
evangelists—the Methodists in particular.

A case in point was Dr. Dodd, a personable, popular
preacher who stirred all London with his superb oratory
and magnetic personality. If Dodd had been an honest,
sincere man, he might have done great good, for he had
the best of credentials. As a royal chaplain and honorary
canon of Brecon, he officiated at the Chapel in Palace
Street, Westminster.

Typical of his kind, he tried to advance his own

position by downgrading others whose success he had reason to covet. While preaching great and accepted truths on the one hand, he took advantage of his reputation and position to make libelous attacks upon the Wesleys, casting grave doubts regarding the underlying purpose of their ministry. John and Charles were deeply disturbed by Dodd's accusations, but wisely refrained from any move toward defense or retaliation. Their faith was strong in the biblical axiom "Be sure your sin will find you out." Surely it would eventually indict the guilty one and clear their names. It did.

First, Dodd tried to bribe the Lord Chancellor's wife to procure for him the rectorship of the much-sought-after St. Georges Church, Hanover Square. Soon after this breach of ethics became known, it was discovered that he had forged the name of Lord Chesterfield on a bill involving a large amount of money. For this, he was condemned to die. On death row, waiting to be hanged, Dodd sought forgiveness for his sins and asked that he might be allowed a visit by the Reverend John Wesley for whom he secretly held great respect. John, responding to the call, became instrumental in assisting his old opponent to repent and accept the gracious forgiveness of God.

John's dedication to the revival never waned. He would "spend and be spent in it" as long as strength of limb and clarity of mind possessed him. This was his calling.

Charles's dedication was no less profound than that of his brother, but his situation was different. As long as he was needed, he gave full time to the work of an evangelist. Now, six years after his mother's death, he discovered that he was a lonely man facing forty. He longed for peace and comfort, a wife and children with whom he could make a home—*home* with all the bliss and beauty that lovely word inspires—and loved ones to share with him a pastoral ministry while he wrote his sacred songs.

This dream was not impossible. Younger men were becoming available to relieve him of his itinerant ministry. It may have seemed that his chance for a healthy, happy home life had passed him by. Or, perhaps, he himself had passed up all such opportunities. Where could he find a companion now of proper age and desires who would share his life and ministry? No scarcity of eligible women existed, but a purely "convenience marriage" was an abomination to Charles Wesley. Marriage to him was the most sacred, serious sacrament the early church fathers had devised.

Charles was always popular with women. He had been dodging female admirers from the days of his youth at Oxford and Stanton when Betty Kirkham had been unable to hide her attraction for him. He was not a woman hater, but he was particular. To make a successful union, he believed, a husband and wife must be compatible in age, background, circumstances, and station in life—with genuine affection interwoven with a mutual love of God. Nothing less would meet the necessary criterion. *In my case,* he mused sadly, *matrimony is out of the question.*

Then he met Sally Gwynne.

Sally was the daughter of a wealthy Welsh magistrate, Marmaduke Gwynne, who owned a large country mansion—known as Garth—in Brecknockshire, South Wales. He and his excellent wife had reared nine children and maintained a domestic chaplain and twenty servants. The couple and at least some of their children had been converted under the ministry of an evangelist named Howell Harris, whom Justice Gwynne had gone to hear, intending to cause his arrest. Charles Wesley met Marmaduke Gwynne at Bristol in 1745.

Sally Gwynne was a studious young lady whom her parents had considered worthy of a liberal education. From her early childhood, tutors were hired to teach her. She had made the most of opportunities; not only was she well versed in the classics and history, but she had developed a love for music. Mature, quiet, pensive, and pretty, Sally appeared old for her twenty years. Young men of her social set tried in vain to win her special attention. She treated them all alike—showing neither favoritism nor interest beyond that of neighbor and friend.

Then she met Charles Wesley.

In his travels, Charles was visiting a clergyman friend who lived about two miles from Garth. Two years before, Mr. Gwynne had met Charles at Bristol, and having liked the serious evangelist, remembered him well. Upon hearing that Wesley was in the community, Gwynne went to meet him with Sally and another daughter.

"Please come to Garth and preach," he begged. "We always have a number of houseguests who, along with my family and our workers, will provide you with an audience—much smaller, of course, but perhaps as good as those you are accustomed to facing."

Charles remained a guest at Garth for six delightful days. He preached, sang, recited his verses, and fell hopelessly in love with Sally. All his former prejudices concerning marriage melted away like the mists of dawn. He was twenty years her senior. She was rich; he was poor. Servants were always at her command; Charles washed his own clothes when on the road between appointments. He dared not allow anyone, especially Sally, to guess his feelings; they were that ridiculous.

But what about Sally? She had fallen in love with Charles. She, too, hid her feelings from everyone, especially Mr. Wesley, as she always called him. She was certain that all her friends, even Charles, would laugh aloud if they so much as guessed the truth.

Nevertheless, just before Charles left the Gwynne's beautiful mansion for a preaching tour of Ireland, he and Sally enjoyed a long, serious conversation. Both were strangely evasive. Charles told her of the lonely days and nights he spent when only his love of God sustained him. Sally warned him of the dangers he incurred by rising too early and working too late without diversion.

"You must take care of your health, Charles. . . ." The girl blushed crimson, having accidentally addressed the minister so informally.

"It's all right," he said, in an effort to ease her embarrassment. "I'm always happy when my close friends call me Charles."

A bridge between two hearts was under construction. "I love to receive letters," the girl spoke softly. "If you were to write to me from Ireland, I would be highly honored."

"If you promise to answer by return post," he countered, "I'll gladly do it."

Through the ensuing correspondence, Charles and Sally confessed their love for one another, but no reference to marriage or the future was made. Charles talked at length with John, explaining the strange affair in the making. John, who was infatuated with a pretty lady himself, was noncommittal.

"There are dangers involved, of course," said John. "But you have always understood women better than anyone I know. I can only trust your judgment in the matter."

Charles sailed from Dublin on a windy October morning after preaching daily for two long months up and down the Emerald Isle. After crossing a treacherous Irish sea, he rode horseback through a chilly rain down across Wales, arriving finally at Garth, spent and running a fever. No better care could he have gotten at the finest clinic in London than was his to enjoy with the Gwynnes. And no nurse in all the commonwealth could have given him the tender, loving care he received from Sally.

"I must get up and dress and be about my work," Charles explained the second day of his visit. "I can't lie in bed forever."

But Sally flatly refused to bring his clothes. "Not until your fever is broken," she answered firmly. "A backset now will leave you worse than ever."

"But I have important things to talk about with you," he complained. "I have been looking forward to our walking together alone through the garden and sitting beneath the trees whenever the autumn wind and rain are ready to cooperate."

"The wind and rain have ceased," said Sally. "The day is warm and beautiful. Now, I'm going to fetch a chair and sit quietly by your side. While we pretend we are in the garden, I'll listen to everything you have to say."

When the lovely lass was seated, she took his hand and smiled down into his eyes. Now Charles was ill at ease and blushingly embarrassed. He hesitated.

"Why don't you just go ahead and ask me? I'm dying to say, 'I will,'" she said. And she flashed the prettiest smile he had ever seen.

The lovers kept their secret for several days while Charles, who had fully recovered from his illness, prepared to ask Marmaduke Gwynne for his daughter's hand in marriage. Neither Charles nor Sally had any inkling as to what the parents' reaction to the stunning news would be. And it might have come as a shock indeed to the older generation except that Sally's younger sister, Becky, saw through the whole affair.

"Teenagers," Sally said later, "have a strange sixth sense, which they lose when they get old and smart."

Becky, realizing that Charles would probably be a poor man always, feared her folks might raise serious objections to such an unusual union. She secretly took the matter to her mother.

"Have no fears, my daughter," the good woman said with a pleasant smile, putting her arm around the girl. "Your father and I are fond of the little minister who has brought happiness and peace into our lives. Yes, a problem is to be resolved, but be assured, dear girl, that I would rather give your sister to Mr. Wesley than to any man in England."

Marmaduke concurred when Charles nervously asked him for Sally's hand. The problem Mrs. Gwynne had referred to was a practical one: *Could Charles provide 100 pounds a year to support a wife?* (This was considered well above the poverty level of that day.) He could. His songs were being purchased, and John assisted him with funds from book sales.

Six months later, on April 8, 1749, Charles Wesley and Sally Gwynne were united in marriage by brother John. In writing about the happy event, Charles reported as follows: "Not a cloud was to be seen from morning till night. I rose at four, spent three hours and a half in prayer or singing. . . . At eight, I led *my Sally* to the church.

"Mr. Gwynne gave her to me (under God): my brother joined our hands. It was a most solemn season of love! Never had I more of the divine presence at the sacrament. We sang together:

> Come, thou everlasting Lord,
> By our trembling hearts adored;
> Come, thou heaven-descended Guest
> Bidden to the marriage feast!"

Sally was a true soldier of the cross. She moved out of the mansion Garth to a humble rented house in Bristol with never a word of complaint. She took part in meetings immediately, playing the harpsichord and singing her husband's hymns with voice and spirit as beautiful as the inspired words of which she was justly proud.

Then came the day when Charles was forced to prepare for the road again.

"I'm sorry to leave you for a season, Sally," he said, "but a two-month trip—a hard one to be sure—demands my presence. I will miss you terribly, but by the end of June, I shall return."

"Aren't you going to ask me to go along?" she asked.

"I can't ask you to do that," he said. "The long days on horseback, rowdies throwing stones and rotten eggs while I am preaching, and the miserable nights in all kinds of places makes even the thought of it impossible. I'm sorry. But soon I'll discontinue my field responsibility. We will live like man and wife are supposed to live—at home together."

"I'm going with you," she said. "Shall I try to carry my harpsichord?"

Amazingly, this young woman, who had been reared

in luxury, adapted readily to the hardship of the road. The people loved her. Even the rowdies were less vehement, aiming their missiles at other targets when she stood by her husband's side. She was a blessing to the women who sought counsel and a nurse to the sick and injured. She gave loving care to a boy who for excitement had engaged in the persecution. He lay bleeding from the nose and from an ugly gash on the upper arm following a skirmish. Who had hurt him no one knew, but the lad thought one of the rowdies mistook him for a Methodist. Sally assisted him to his home where his parents, who had violently opposed the revival, were stricken with conviction and later were converted. The boy, Mark Mariville, eventually became a leader of one of the societies.

Charles and Sally returned to Bristol. They launched another campaign at Cornwall, then worked their way northward for seven weeks of travel and travail. This was Sally's last, hard trip with her husband, for she discovered en route that their first child was on the way.

Charles, as promised, gave up the road to devote his time to pastoring, to assisting the young men who felt called to the ministry, to the never-ending task of writing sacred verse, and to his family, whom he loved second only to the Christ he served so well.

By 1750, Charles Wesley had written nearly a thousand songs. One of his contemporaries, Isaac Watts, likewise heralded in all Christendom as among the great in creating religious verse, honored Charles by saying, "That single poem, 'Wrestling Jacob,' is worth all the verses I have ever written."

CHAPTER XIV

John, Grace, and Molly

In Susanna's death, son John lost more than a loving parent; he also lost a friend. Never again could he kneel at her feet, feel her loving touch, or call upon her counsel to unburden his troubled mind and soul.

His loneliness was partially lost in the never-relaxing load the revival pressed upon him. Onward through life he pursued his course: riding, writing, reading, teaching, preaching, praying, and building a fellowship of believers that would reach "to the uttermost part of the earth."

But his loneliness surfaced at the close of every busy day. From the moment he laid his head upon the pillow till he relaxed enough to fall asleep, he longed for the bridge of minds and hearts he and Susanna had maintained throughout her life. As long as he knew she was praying for his safety and success, waiting patiently for his return, he had endured the lonely times with a measure of comfort.

After several vain attempts to find another Susanna to

be his wife, John simply assumed that the celibate life was his to endure. He had little difficulty ignoring a desire for anything more than ordinary female fellowship until brother Charles married lovely Sally Gwynne. That happy union succeeded in changing John's mind completely. Slowly the lonely hours became times of pleasant fantasying—searching for a companion to share his hectic, itinerant life. And twice again he thought he had found her.

The first object of John's new romantic dreams was Grace Murray, a thirty-two-year-old widow. Several months before Charles and Sally Gwynne were married, Mrs. Murray had nursed John through a siege of sickness involving a devastating, blinding headache. From all that John could learn, Grace Murray, who earlier had been a vacillating Christian, now possessed every trait and talent he or any minister might hope for in marriage. Surely she was the other Susanna for whom he searched.

Twelve years earlier, Grace had married Alexander Murray, a sailor—a ship's captain—whose long sea voyages left her lonely and sad. Two babies came and went the way of all flesh, one through miscarriage, leaving her despondent to the point of near distraction.

A friend persuaded her to go to Moorsfield to hear a little Methodist evangelist preach the unsearchable riches of Christ. She listened to his message of hope and heard him cry, "Is there anyone here who has a true desire to be saved?" Grace Murray said, "My heart replied, *I have—oh, yes, I have.*" Several months later, the lonely lady was converted and joined the Methodists.

Alexander Murray, returning home in 1742, at first

opposed his wife in what he considered a vain, offensive fanaticism. Before he left, though, he came to agree that her salvation was real. Only heaven knows if he, too, became a Christian.

On his next voyage, Murray's boat capsized. Grace, upon receiving word that her husband had drowned, entered an extended season of mourning. Then she returned to her hometown of Newcastle more than two hundred miles north of Bristol. There, to her delight, she saw a building under construction by the Methodists.

Shortly after Susanna's death, John Wesley had preached with marked success at Newcastle. Upon announcing his wish to build a preaching place there, a wealthy merchant offered a plot of ground—forty-eight by ninety feet—in exchange for a token payment. Then a Quaker friend sent John a check for 100 pounds (probably equal to thousands of dollars in today's inflated economy) with which to purchase material for the building. When completed, the new edifice was called the Orphan House.

Grace Murray was well aware that Mr. Wesley, whose name was becoming common to the ears of English, Scotch, Welsh, and Irish friends and foes alike, was the little evangelist who had preached her under conviction at Moorsfield years before. She was determined to meet him.

In the early days of the Orphan House, both John and Charles spent much time there—teaching, preaching, and appointing and organizing workers to carry on in their absence. Grace Murray offered her services. This gesture was deeply appreciated by both the Wesleys, for capable workers were hard to find. They appointed her to the overseeing position of housekeeper, but this was not enough for such an ambitious, talented lady as Grace Murray. Soon, without the formality of appointment, she was conducting a class of more than one hundred members. Likewise, visiting and praying with the sick in neighboring villages became a regular part of her self-assumed ministry.

John Wesley was certain that heaven had sent an angel of mercy to lift the load at the Orphan House and expand the work he had begun. Other workers had been appointed, too, of course, but John—during his extended evangelistic tours—depended upon the talented leadership of Grace Murray to keep the "ship afloat" at Newcastle.

When Charles returned from a preaching mission of several months' duration, John fought to find words to adequately convey to him his appreciation for Mrs. Murray.

"Charles," he said, "That dear lady is remarkably neat; nicely frugal, yet not sordid; gifted with a large amount of common sense. Patient and inexpressibly tender, she is quick, cleanly, skillful, and of an engaging behavior. Moreover, she is of a mind sprightly, cheerful and yet serious temper; while lastly, her gifts for usefulness are such as I have not seen equaled."

Charles smiled his amusement at John's elaborate recommendation of their new employee and nodded his momentary agreement. Soon, however, the ever-alert younger brother began to note that the other workers were unhappy—jealous perhaps of their talented superior. Then the good sense with which Charles Wesley was wonderfully endowed began to present another face to the picture. He found opportunities to talk with the girls who worked under Grace Murray's direction. They admitted they were unhappy at Orphan House, but being Christians in word and deed, none would pinpoint the problem or offer a word of criticism. An all-around handyman and janitor—a congenial, hard-working African named Sylvester—finally confirmed Charles's suspicions.

"That Mrs. Murray is the problem," he said. "Don't misunderstand me. She loves the Lord, but she is weak."

"Weak?" asked Charles.

"Yes. That's why she pretends to be strong—always building herself up."

"I see," Charles answered thoughtfully. "She runs down the other workers so all the credit for what is done goes to her."

"Exactly," Sylvester answered. "She's mean to the others when no one's watching. Mr. Wesley doesn't know it, but all the girls are trying to find work other places."

"It's that bad, aye?" asked Charles.

"I'm sorry, sir," Sylvester said with a note of remorse. "I shouldn't have talked like that. It just slipped out because I know all the workers are doing their best."

"It's all right, my good man," said Charles. "I'll not quote you to my brother or anyone. But I will see what I can do to correct the situation."

"Thank you, Mister Charles," the black man responded with genuine appreciation. "I'm sure you will. I'm just sure you will."

Convincing John of his misplaced confidence was not an easy task for the younger brother. Several times, Charles tried in vain to open the subject. Then came an unexpected answer to the problem. One of Wesley's preachers was taken suddenly, seriously ill. John had him fetched to the Orphan House, where one of the girls with nursing experience attended him. The second day the ailing man began to show marked improvement; his recovery seemed assured. Then Grace Murray attempted to take over the care of the invalid, but the nurse refused to give up her charge. Harsh words ensued until Charles stepped in to referee the bout. Fortunately, John was gone for the day.

Charles quietly, kindly, but with a note of finality, told Grace to return to her duties. Instead, she left in a huff and went to live with her mother. But after six months, she returned to Orphan House, and John rehired her. Soon a problem similar to the former one developed and, upon receiving another reprimand, she took her wounded pride and made her way back to her mother again.

In the language of the Wesleys, Grace Murray fell from grace. Certainly she slipped into a period of spiritual darkness and mental depression. For two years she remained in seclusion. Then, having regained her health, she renewed her covenant with God, rejoined the Methodists, and humbly asked permission to return to her work. This time she kept her place and managed to get along with others.

By then, a nurse was greatly needed at Orphan House. Grace Murray was assigned immediately to serve in this capacity. She ministered to as many as seven of Wesley's overworked itinerant preachers with each of whom she artfully established a secret affection.

One of those preachers was John Bennet, a special friend of both the Wesleys. Bennet was under Mrs. Murray's care for six long months, during which time the "harmless" little affection ballooned. A deep infatuation developed. It may not have culminated in a full-fledged engagement, but an informal pledge to marry at some future convenient date was solemnly made by the lovers. Whether the other patients and workers were fully aware of this is not known, but a gossipy cook at Orphan House was heard to say, "That Murray widow is a flirt—nothing but a flirt."

Such was the lady who turned the head of John Wesley. In 1748, when she was caring for him through his bout with his blinding headaches, he became convinced that she was the "Susanna" for whom he longed. Her tender, loving care and winsome smile was all the convincing proof he needed; he was that naive. He recovered slowly from his illness, the final day of which he confessed his love to her and proposed marriage all in one long sentence.

Grace Murray was taken by surprise. She had been using every wile and winning way she possessed to attract her patient's attention, but she hadn't guessed how well she had succeeded.

"This is too great a blessing to me," she stammered. For once she felt that she was not in control. "I cannot tell how to believe it. This is all I could have wished for under heaven!"

With that brief exchange, another "eternal triangle" was created—Wesley and Bennet at the bottom angles, Grace Murray at the apex, and Satan in the middle, grinning his delight. If Charles Wesley hadn't been so deeply involved with his own love affair, he might have foreseen the development and saved his brother from one of the most unfortunate experiences of his life.

But Charles was involved in his own love drama

which, unlike John's, was "right" from every angle. During the three and a half months he and his bride pursued the itinerant trail together, they were out of touch with John and unaware of his developing romance with Grace Murray. But they learned of it when they reached Epworth, where Charles had arranged for the post to hold his mail.

Not one, but five letters were waiting to inform Charles of his brother's unwise, unbelievable, but apparently successful attempt to woo a woman—a widow— already duly promised to his friend and coworker, Mr. Bennet. And that wasn't all. John Wesley, the missives read, had taken Mrs. Murray with him on an extended tour of Ireland, providing fodder for the mill of nasty rumors already being spread by the unbridled gossiping tongues of Newcastle. Ironically, four of the five letters were from the unbridled, gossiping pens of just such disturbers of truth who bristled with ulterior motives of their own. The fifth message was from a friend of both John and Charles who feared the consequences of the affair.

"Please come to Bristol at your earliest convenience," the note read. "I will fill you in on all the details, hoping that you can be used of God in the solving of a problem that is freighted with potential to destroy the work that is progressing so well." He signed the note, "Your brother and friend in the Gospel, Tom McMasters."

Tom McMasters, a professional tutor who assisted young men in preparing for college entrance, was a lay worker—one of the original class leaders appointed at the suggestion of Captain Foy in the early days at Bristol. Tom was an unpretentious fellow who worked behind the scenes, always at his post. Both John and Charles depended upon his cautious judgment and often sought his advice, knowing that he would keep their counsel. The letter Tom sent to Charles was doubly important, for it marked the first time this quiet soldier of the cross had offered an opinion that hadn't been requested.

Charles was angry with the news of John's unfortunate involvement with Grace Murray. He trusted neither John's judgment nor Grace's motives. He remembered with disgust John's deliberate attempt to win the hand of Sally Kirkham, knowing that she was engaged to marry the local schoolmaster. Charles was aware that Grace Murray had been a housemaid—one of the serving class, a long step below the social level of the sons of Epworth rectory. He was anxious to know what further facts in the unsavory situation were forthcoming from Tom McMasters. He didn't have to wait long.

"I'm sorry I have to involve myself in this matter which ordinarily would come under the heading of 'none of my business,'" said Tom. He and Charles had found a quiet nook to discuss the subject at hand.

"I understand you," Charles answered. "Once again, I fear I am about to be placed in the embarrassing position of being *big* brother to my *elder* brother."

"An embarrassing position to be sure," said Tom. "I kept completely out of the picture until nasty rumors of immorality incriminating your brother and Mrs. Murray reached my ears. I didn't believe them, of course, but I soon became aware that some of John's best friends were being influenced by the gossip. I knew then that not only would John's good character be irreparably damaged, but the work to which he is giving his life might be lost in the process. It was then I began an investigation of my own."

Tom rose nervously from his chair and walked to a

window. For several moments he quietly looked out upon the street below. Talking behind the back of his best friend was as foreign to Tom's quiet nature as anything he might imagine. Charles feared his informant was about to change his mind and keep his findings to himself.

Then Tom returned. "If I believed anything amiss in John's conduct, I would hold my peace," he said. "But since I'm certain he is as innocent as a kitten, my silence would harm him immeasurably, and I would share the blame."

"Go on," said Charles. "I have to know the whole story."

"It simmers down to this," Tom continued. "Should I believe that John and Grace are in love, I would beg you to get them to the altar. But real love—between one man and one woman—does not exist in their case."

"I believe that," said Charles, "but I am anxious to know your reason for thinking so."

"If Grace loves any man, it is Bennet," said Tom. "In the very midst of her planning to marry your brother, she wrote to him saying she believed she must return her affections to Bennet after all. Real love would never abide that. Then John's response was equally revealing. He said simply that, in such case, perhaps she should do it. Real love is never as subdued as that either."

"Why didn't that end the romance?" asked Charles.

"Well, Mrs. Murray sees John as the better catch. Bennet will never be more than a second-rate pastor, and Grace Murray knows it. So she continued to correspond with both men. She even allowed Bennet to read John's most intimate letters. Then she accepted John's innocent invitation to accompany him to Ireland. They're back now and John is waiting for an opportunity to see

Bennet face-to-face to satisfy him regarding the taking away of his promised bride. He's waiting for you also. No doubt he wants you to perform the nuptial rites."

"He will wait a long time," said Charles. "I don't fully understand my brother," he went on. "He must *think* he loves the lady."

"Of course he does, but it's not Grace Murray that he loves," said Tom. "It's the memory of his mother. He has said that Mrs. Murray cares for his every need exactly as his loving parent always did."

Tom paused; Charles waited. It seemed as natural as life that the speaker had not conveyed all that he was thinking. He hadn't, but in one short sentence, Tom reached his conclusion.

"Men marry their sweethearts, not their mothers," he said with conviction.

Charles met John a few days later at Whitehaven, where his words of warning went unheeded. Next he went to see Mrs. Murray and rode with her to Newcastle. There they met with Bennet. No one knows exactly what Charles told them, but within a week Bennet and Grace were wed.

How did John Wesley respond to that? At first the shock was hard to bear. Several days later, John met the newlyweds in the presence of Charles, George White-field, and a friend, John Nelson. In these embarrassing, highly emotional moments Whitefield and Nelson prayed and wept. Then John embraced Bennet without a word of unfriendly nature and congratulated him and his terribly embarrassed bride.

Charles, in private interview with John, entirely exon-erated him, laying all the blame on the fickle lady who had won, then destroyed his affection. But John knew in his heart that he, too, carried blame for his susceptibility.

John wrote a note to a friend, Thomas Bigg, in Newcastle: "Since I was six years old I never met with such a severe trial. . . . The fatal stroke was struck on Tuesday last. Yesterday I saw my friend (that was) and him to whom she is sacrificed. I believe you never saw such a scene. 'But why should a living man complain, man for the punishment of his sins?'"

To unload his burden, John—in typical Wesley style—opened his heart to the world in thirty-one, six-line stanzas entitled "Reflections upon Past Providences." The following verse reflects his feeling:

> Oft, as through giddy youth I roved,
> And danced along the flowery way,
> By chance or thoughtless passions moved,
> An easy, unresisting prey,
> I fell, while love's envenomed dart
> Thrilled through my nerves and tore my heart.

As to the other players in the drama, John Bennet left his charge and opened an independent church. He took 108 members of his Methodist congregation with him. In vain he tried to destroy the Wesleys, constantly accusing them from the pulpit of false motives and all manner of transgressions. He preached a compromising gospel, all to no avail. The work apparently died in his hands. He then accepted a pastorate at Warburton near Warrington with another group, whose doctrinal position was at odds with Methodism.

John Bennet died when he was forty-five, leaving his widow with five small boys. Grace Murray Bennet conducted meetings for prayer and fellowship while rearing her family well. She rejoined the Methodists and one of her boys became a minister. She met John Wesley only once again—in 1788—when he was eighty-five years old. She died in 1803 in her eighty-sixth year.

John Wesley's final love affair ended in marriage and disaster. This time also the woman in his life was a widow, Molly Vazeille. The wedding took place in February 1751, when John was forty-seven.

Mrs. Vazeille was a woman of considerable wealth and the mother of at least two children. She had recently made the acquaintance of Charles and Sally Wesley who, for a short period, at least, became her friends. She needed a man, not for his money but for warm, close companionship. She had reached the broad plains of middle life.

John's relationship with Molly Vazielle started with an accident. London streets were a glare of ice. John, hurrying to his next appointment, was crossing London Bridge when he slipped and fell, striking his ankle on a sharp stone. He feared the bone was broken. He was carried to the home of Mrs. Vazielle in Threadneedle Street. The lady offered to care for him during his convalescence.

"Call me Molly," she said as she carefully dressed the swollen ankle that was causing excruciating pain. She was a strong, good-looking woman—not beautiful in a physical sense, but good-looking.

John was a perfect patient. No word of complaint escaped him. Molly saw in John a perfect husband: one who needed her—needed her money, too, she thought.

She perceived him to be a mild little man who would bow to her every whim. Here was one who would share her life, her bed, and her ambitions. With him, she could rule, and rule she must.

Her fantasy was one of perfection—so different from the memory of her first marriage with a husband who accepted his role as head of the house with vigor. He had held the purse strings, being a man of commerce who knew how to make money and save it. She had maintained an all-too-common love-hate relationship with him. He had died early, leaving her a veritable fortune of 10,000 pounds—enough that she might live comfortably the rest of her life. But she needed more than money. And she was certain she had found it in a quiet little man with a swollen ankle.

John saw in Molly a caring person whose tender touch and soothing words were everything he needed—a perfect companion to keep his house and share his burdens. He believed she would patiently wait and pray for his safe return from fields afar, even as his mother had done. Then she would counsel him in matters great and small. Surely this was the Susanna of his search.

But certain fears in the area of matrimony possessed John Wesley. Misgivings regarding the marriage state had always harassed him. Now he was a forty-seven-year-old bachelor, whose ideal among all the world of women had always been Susanna, the "perfect" example. Men with a mother fixation tend to possess guilt feelings regarding the marriage bed. Sigmund Freud, who might have helped John Wesley, was yet a hundred years unborn. John reasoned, *I am not choosing a twenty-year-old girl as did my brother Charles but a woman beyond the romantic age.*

And Molly's money, which many men would have

looked upon as reason enough to seek her favor, presented another problem to the man who looked upon worldly wealth as an abomination—the love of which the Bible says is "the root of all evil." He surmounted this hurdle, promising himself to be certain that Molly's temporal assets were safely locked in her name only, if indeed she would become his wife.

With the above matters settled (in his own mind), John Wesley proposed marriage to Molly Vazielle while still in her care. She, of course, accepted. They were married February 18, 1751.

Charles opposed this union with stronger conviction than any of his brother's former ventures toward matrimony. First, he had come to doubt that John could ever be happily married. Second, he and Sally were agreed that while the ambitious Molly Vazeille was in the market for a man, John was searching for a mother. They didn't need a sage to spell out the impending problems.

The honeymoon was a strange one. John, hobbling along with a crutch; Molly, spending money like a youngster who had just found a bulging wallet on her way from school. The rest can only be surmised. Cool-headed John was willing to take any unsatisfactory relationship in stride, making the most of it. Hot-headed Molly allowed her disappointment to develop into an emotional state that someday would border on insanity.

Two weeks after the wedding, John, still needing help in mounting his steed, made a hurried trip to Bristol. Charles and Sally did their best to make the strange union bearable. Taking advantage of John's absence, they paid the unhappy Molly a friendly visit in London. She was appreciative and kind, not mentioning the nature of the incompatible relationship that was developing between herself and the husband she was coming to realize she hardly knew. During that visit Sally spoke privately to her husband, "This Molly is a conundrum. She gives every appearance of being religious, but I'm beginning to fear it is all pretense. I don't like to be judgmental, but I wonder if she has a spark of grace."

John's preconceived idea of a wife waiting and praying for his safe return from months in the field, failed, of course, to find favor with Molly. And since his bowing to her every whim was pure fantasy, she was determined to buy herself a horse and ride along with him, adopting a life-style unlike anything she had ever known. The trails they rode were hard, bumpy, and extremely tiresome. The places they found to stay overnight were primitive, poor, and unkempt. Rowdies, disrupting the services, filled Molly with fear and anger. Women, whom John considered sisters in Christ—nothing more —were forever approaching her for counsel in which the wealthy, worldly Molly had no experience whatever. Nor did she have any desire to obtain it. And she resented John's interest in these women as he listened to their woes and comforted them with words of wisdom and Christian love. But nothing disturbed her more than the one who bragged about the other Mrs. Wesley, saying, "Sally, dear soul, helped me through a time of trial and trouble."

After four months of travel, John and Molly Wesley rode into Bristol. Charles and Sally welcomed them with open arms. Sally sensed a coldness in Molly she hadn't felt before. She mentioned it to Charles who, always alert, had noticed it, too.

"We want to help them," Sally said. "I'll treat her like

the friend she has always been, but I'll leave the counseling to you."

John's room, which he maintained at Bristol, was adequate but cold and poorly furnished. There Charles found his sister-in-law alone in tears. "I wish to help you, Molly," he said. "If you have a problem, why not share it? I'll keep your counsel and help you if I can."

Molly Wesley poured out her heart to Charles, holding back only a little as she enumerated her complaints against John. Charles listened; there was little else he could do. But the next day he met with Molly and John together and saw the two reach as near a peaceful understanding as was ever possible in the whole twenty years of their militant, married life.

For four long years the strange couple rode the itinerant trail; then Molly cried, "Enough!" Why she traveled so rugged a way she hated with a vengeance throughout a whole quadrennium is an unanswered question, but it does speak well for Molly. Why John put up with her incessant nagging and complaints is equally astounding, speaking well for him. When he traveled alone, her jealous anger became an obsession. She became suspicious of his every move, every friend. She convinced herself that others were receiving from John the very attentions for which she craved. As her emotional problem became a serious malady, she sometimes took a carriage a hundred miles or more to an upcoming preaching point to spy on him, to ascertain who might be his traveling companion.

Periodically, she packed her bag and left the home that her husband admittedly occupied too seldom. Later, she would return unexpectedly to search his clothing and desk for letters in hope of substantiating her suspicions. In a spirit of revenge, she confiscated accounts, important correspondence, legal papers, and particularly, pages of his journal. On one occasion she dragged John across the room by his long wavy locks, pulling some of them out by the roots.

John, for a variety of reasons, failed as a husband. This was obvious, but few people blamed him. He never allowed his matrimonial troubles to hinder his commission to preach the gospel. He had told his evangelists that he could not understand how a Methodist preacher could answer it to God to preach one sermon or travel one mile less in a married state than in a single state. He had said the same to Molly before their marriage. She had concurred, saying to herself, no doubt, *I'll handle that*. But she severely underestimated John's strength of will. He kept the rule religiously as the revival rolled on, carrying him farther from her every passing month.

When John and Molly were both at home, she could have been a great help to him. Among other things, she might have entertained his associates, but she refused to allow them to enter the door. After eight long years of unhappy marriage, John wrote Molly a letter in which he enumerated the faults and shortcomings he found in her, hoping to find a way to some kind of understanding.

Among other things, he wrote, "I dislike not having command of my own house, not being at liberty to invite even my nearest relations to drink a dish of tea. . . . My home is not my castle. I cannot call my study, even my bureau, my own. . . . You forget even good breeding and use such coarse language as befits none but a fishwife." On and on he laid her faults upon the line. This, of course, did not ease the strain or militate in favor of reconciliation.

John Wesley never failed to take a philosophical view of even the worst of circumstances. He was heard to say,

John, Grace, and Molly

"I believe that God overruled this prolonged sorrow for my good. If Mrs. Wesley had been a better wife, I might have been unfaithful to my work."

A letter dated 1771 indicates that after twenty years Molly still spent at least a part of her time with her husband. Soon after that she left home, never to return. She died at Camberwell in 1781. "On October 14," John wrote, "I came to London and was informed that my wife died on Monday. . . . She was buried, though I was not informed of it until a day or two after."

CHAPTER XV

"Tribulation Worketh Patience"

The decade of the 1750s opened in London with a blast. A major earthquake struck the city on February 8, sending people into the streets. Fear of aftershocks kept everyone alert for days, but since nothing of consequence followed for several weeks, the hysteria ended.

Then, one month to the day from the first quake, came another. This second shock, much more violent than the first, struck in the darkness of early dawn while the city slept. Fallen chimneys, buckled buildings, uprooted trees, and terrified screams of the maimed and dying brought horror, then panic, to the metropolis second only to the devastating fire of 1666. Hundreds of people who hadn't attended a religious service in years were wailing in prayer—dreading the judgment of God. With one exception, fear of falling blocks and timbers kept the people out in the open air. Only the churches were suddenly packed to the walls.

Charles Wesley had ridden into London the day before

the second quake. He stayed at the foundry. As usual, he arose early and was busily writing another hymn. A number of early risers had entered the room and begged for a sermon to start the day. Charles took a text when suddenly the narrow desk at which he was sitting over-turned. Simultaneously, a weird roar sounded and the rattle of breaking dishes reached him from the scullery. For a moment, the walls of the ancient building trembled like a reed.

Charles dropped to his knees and prayed with fervor—not for himself, but for the thousands of unsaved souls in the wicked city. He paused momentarily to thank the Lord that Sally and their first little daughter were safe in bed in Bristol 120 miles away. The doors of the foundry were bolted, but soon a frantic pounding of fists on both windows and doors arrested the praying preacher's attention. He allowed the frightened hoards to enter the building, exhorting all to seek the mercy of God.

The tragic quake had a ballooning effect upon the revival. But Charles said later that, *to him,* the earthshak-ing experience was like a warning of evil things to come. Certainly the decade of the fifties was a period of misunderstanding, trials, and sorrows for the singular songster of Methodism.

By the middle of 1753, Charles and Sally had wept over the caskets of their first four babies whose names are unknown. The bearing and losing of these jewels from heaven had left their marks upon the mother. Fine wrinkles appeared around her eyes and mouth which friends kindly explained, "only enhance your beauty." She smiled her appreciation, saying, "Surely God will forgive you for stretching the truth a little, since you are trying to help me."

Then the lovely Sally was stricken with smallpox—the most radical type of the malady. Ugly scabs covered her body, reached into her hair and left in their wake the most horrid of pockmarks, deep and indelible. In a matter of days, they stole away her beauty and youth forever.

Charles suffered with her moment by moment. Only his unwavering affection sustained her. Their marriage had been one of genuine appreciation and deep, abiding love. Nothing could change that. During the long hours of her delirium, Charles sat by her side, keeping her nails trimmed and her fingers wrapped in cloths to protect the sores as she fought to relieve the itching that nearly drove her to distraction.

Finally the fever receded, and Sally was on the road to recovery. One rainy morning she was sleeping peacefully through the early hours when Charles asked Mary, a servant girl, to take his place by her bed. He went to his room for badly needed rest. When Sally awoke, the early light of day filled the sickroom. She studied the scars on her hands and arms and felt of her face and shoulders. She asked for Charles.

"Your husband is sound asleep," the girl told her. "He has been with you here throughout your illness. You have a good husband, ma'am. He must love you very, very much. Is there anything I can do to help you?"

"Yes, Mary," she answered. "Please bring me a glass. I want to see my face."

"Ma'am, I think your husband should bring the glass when he awakes. Do you mind waiting? I'm sure he would want it that way."

"All right," said Sally. "I'll try to sleep some more. When I awaken again, please bring him to me."

Charles entered the room, carrying a mirror that he laid on a bedside table. "I brought the glass, dear," he said. "Are you sure you are ready to look into it?"

"Yes, Charles," she answered. "Nothing will be gained by waiting."

"First, there is something I must tell you," he said. "Prepare to be shocked at what you see, but remember this: I love you more today than ever in our lives. Your beauty has always come from within. It still does—it always shall. To me, you are more beautiful now than the day we met. The devil will tell you that isn't so, Sally, but he's 'a liar and the father of lies.'"

"Thank you, dear," she answered. "I believe you."

Charles held the glass before her. She fought to contain her tears. Charles, sensing the depth of her emotions, was the most miserable of men. Then, winning the battle, Sally's remarkable sense of humor came to their rescue.

"There's one good thing," she said. "No stranger again will mistake me for your daughter."

Charles explained later to his sister Kezzie that out of the tragedy of Sally's illness came a deepening of those precious elements which make a marriage everything God intended it to be.

In 1757, Sally presented her husband with a boy whom they immediately christened Charles, Jr. He inherited his parents' love for music. By age three, the gifted child was playing his mother's harpsichord, and one year later, he aroused the interest of some of London's great musicians with his singular talent.

When Charles, Jr., was two years old, a baby sister was born. They named her Sarah and called her Sally, that her mother might have a namesake, too. She was always amazingly like her mother. Ironically, smallpox robbed her of her beauty when she was in her teens.

Another baby, unnamed, lived but a little while. In 1766, Sally gave birth to her eighth and final child, a boy named Samuel. This lad proved to be of no less a musical genius than his brother.

Following Sally's tragic illness, Charles forsook the itinerant trail forever. It was well that he did. As the revival spread, John Wesley needed a qualified assistant to oversee the headquarters work at Bristol and London. An added responsibility involved the giving of direction to the lay ministers being appointed to the circuits. Who but Charles could John appoint to such an important assistantship?

Charles was aware that owing to the growing need for workers, some of the new recruits were being sent forth with neither gifts nor sufficient knowledge of the Scriptures to succeed in the work. He had said so, but John had been too busy saving souls to listen. Now that Charles was shouldered with ample authority to deal with the problem, he lost no time getting started. He visited the various societies, talked with the people, and listened to the preachers expound the Word. Most of the men were stalwart, sacrificing Christians called of God to preach the gospel. Charles was lavish in his praise of the men who were "rising to the occasion."

But Charles was appalled at some of the sermons he was hearing. Strange interpretations of the Word and an exaggerated importance of minor points of discipline were common. An occasional moral problem appeared, too. For lack of good leadership, serious divisions in the societies were about to destroy the work in several places.

Charles exerted an iron hand. Kindly but firmly, he asked these men to return to their trades. But those requests were nothing less than ultimatums. Charles ran into trouble. Some of the men whom he dismissed from their pulpits reacted angrily. Each had friends who came to his defense. Their number was comparatively small, but as Tom McMasters remarked, "Militant minorities have been making history from its onset."

The name of Charles Wesley was dragged through the slough of vicious gossip. His enemies said he was fat and lazy, taking an easy way of staying home while his brother faced the rigors of the road. He was prejudiced, they said, dismissing men from their charges because he didn't like them. Since his wife had lost her beauty, he was accused of fraternizing with immoral women. These criticisms and more began to reach the ears of John, who returned immediately to Bristol. He was deeply concerned for he needed more men—not less—to take leadership over the mushrooming communities of believers.

Fortunately, Charles was away when John came riding into town. This gave the latter opportunity to discuss those evil reports with Tom McMasters before facing his brother. Tom defended Charles but, as always, he discussed the problems objectively.

"Any suggestion of Charles's unfaithfulness to Sally is completely unfounded," he said with conviction.

"I know," John answered. "I take no stock in that, you may be sure. But what about his dismissing preachers without due cause?" he asked.

"In my opinion, John, the weeding-out process was

necessary and, for the most part, done fairly with good judgment."

"Do you see any problem worthy of my returning to Bristol?" John asked.

Tom hesitated a moment, then he answered. "If you will forgive me for expressing an adverse opinion, I might suggest that Charles may be undergoing a serious change in his thinking. He is suspicious that aggressive steps toward separation from the mother church are under consideration. Like yourself, Charles is a loyal Anglican as well as a genuine Christian. He has intimated to me that the present greatest need for revival lies within the walls of the established church—not out in the fens."

"That's a contention hard to debate," John answered, "but the Lord has seen fit to call us to the masses. He has blessed our efforts beyond our wildest imagination while the doors of the churches have been slammed in our faces. I have no intention of leaving the church, but I must minister where there is hunger for the gospel and fruit for my labors. I shall reason with Charles when he returns."

John and Charles spent three intense hours together in the chapel. They discussed problems, prayed, reasoned, and finally laughed together. John came through with what victory could be claimed.

Charles, in relating the episode to Sally, concluded with the following observation: "Nearly twenty years ago, John convinced me against my will to go with him to Georgia. I said then, *My brother, who always has the ascendancy over me, persuaded me.* Nothing has changed."

The next several months were good ones as John and Charles worked together in harmony. From that moment, a great deal of study and practice was required of every aspirant to the ministry. Many failed to make the grade. In the new building at Bristol were two podiums, one in back of and above the other. There the students passed or failed their final exams.

The novice took his place in the lower pulpit, read his text, and proceeded to preach a trial sermon before a live audience. In the upper pulpit, looking down upon him, was a seasoned, well-trained minister watching and listening for errors in diction, gesture, posture, and general appearance. When a mistake was made, the critic would stop the preacher, explain his error, and ask him to try again. Such interruptions often occurred many times in the course of the message. If this were not enough to test the nerves and try the patience of a novice, at the back of the auditorium John Wesley himself watched through a curtained window, checking the aspirant's theology.

Wesley, however, was not unkind. In giving his report, he invariably spent most of the time discussing the preacher's strong points. Wesley's preachers loved him. Surprisingly few, after passing the test, failed later in their calling.

Eventually, a problem that had long been gnawing at John's heartstrings began to vie for attention. The Methodist ministers, who were an integral (though unwanted) part of the Church of England, had to be ordained by an Episcopal bishop to administer the Sacrament. Few Methodists were so qualified. While John was not an ordained bishop, it was then that he first toyed with the thought of ordaining pastors himself.

When news of this possibility reached Charles, he

threw up his hands in horror. This would constitute an irrevocable step toward the severance of the Methodists from the established church. Charles was aware that such a radical step might be far in the future, but in his anger, he decided to leave his brother and pursue another route to fulfill his calling.

He and George Whitefield had become good friends again. Charles wrote to George, informing him of his intention. He suggested that he would consider teaming up with Whitefield provided the latter would concur.

The answer Charles received was warm and friendly, though not what he expected. Whitefield said, "My dear, dear brother in the Lord . . . I would not willingly for the world do or say anything that may separate such friends." He went on to say that Charles and John had been so close—their attachment so necessary—for so many long, hard years in the work of the kingdom, that surely only Satan would try to disrupt so great a partnership.

Charles Wesley was soundly and rightly rebuked by Whitefield's frank and levelheaded response to his impulsive letter. John and Charles Wesley continued to work together as the revival gained momentum.

Following the Wesleys' reconciliation with Whitefield, Methodists everywhere were asking, "Who gave in to whom?" The well-trained, clear-thinking Tom McMasters was asked for an opinion by a gathering of Methodists of both persuasions. Tom was a teacher, not a preacher. In his calm, logical, scholarly fashion, he faced the issue.

"Neither George Whitefield nor John Wesley found it necessary to yield to the other in their search for common ground upon which to preach the gospel," he stated firmly.

"Mr. Whitefield refers to his theology as the *doctrine of grace*. He preaches election and contends that a sinner, following his acceptance of Christ, ought by all means to give himself to good works and spiritual growth.

"John Wesley," Tom continued, "agrees with Mr. Whitefield that salvation is by grace, through faith. He places strong emphasis on the importance of good works, both in reaching for and maintaining that faith once it is received. Holiness unto the Lord—*perfect love*—is an experience in grace that he contends every Christian should seek with all diligence.

"Both men claim they have ample Scriptures to document their positions. To me, the important thing is that God continues to bless the labors of both men with revival as long as their converts—numbering now in multiplied thousands—grow in grace and knowledge."

McMasters closed his analysis with a final word of warning. "Controversy raises its ugly head when you and I—fruit of the great awakening—return to our evil ways. Since these great leaders have risen above their opposing opinions and are sharing their pulpits again, may God help us to consider those points in which they concur rather than spend ourselves laboring over their differences."

In 1769, George Whitefield made his seventh and final trip to America. Under his leadership, the revival in the colonies had taken on great momentum. Before leaving England, he made it clear that he had been called to do the work of an evangelist. Uniting and motivating the converts to perpetuate the movement for future generations was not his forte. This important phase of the work he must leave to John Wesley, whose talent for organization was seldom equaled in the history of the Christian church.

Whitefield's welcome to Georgia was overwhelming. The orphanage he had built near Savannah was prospering—the debt he incurred on the building was practically eliminated—and two new rooms had been added. The governor received him with public honors. He preached up and down the colonies with unprecedented success. To Charles Wesley, who even during the days of their controversy remained his special friend, he wrote, "I can only sit down and cry, 'What hath God wrought?' My bodily health is much improved, and my soul is on the wing for another Gospel range. Unutterable love! I am lost in wonder and amazement!"

Then one sad night, after having preached two hours to a most enthusiastic crowd at Newsburyport, George Whitefield was stricken with asthma. At six o'clock in the morning, the great orator of Methodism entered eternal rest. Back in England, John Wesley preached the funeral sermon according to the solemn promise the two friends had made each other in days gone by.

The old foundry was deteriorating fast by 1776. A new building, representative of the mushrooming Methodist movement, had become a necessity. And the fact that Whitefield's followers had already erected a beautiful, commodious auditorium only a little distance away made it seem all the more important. John promoted the project.

By 1778, a beautiful house of worship which he called City Road Chapel was erected not far from the foundry, across the road from Bunnhill Fields where Susanna was buried. John described the new house of worship:

> It is perfectly neat, but not fine, and contains far more than the foundry; I believe, together with the morning chapel, as many as the Tabernacle. Many were afraid that the multitudes, crowding from all parts, would have occasioned much disturbance; but they were happily disappointed; there was none at all: all was quietness, decency, and order.

Beside the chapel (No. 47, City Road) stood a residence in which John Wesley made his home. By then, Charles had moved to London. Sally received an inheritance, making it possible for her family to be comfortably situated although its income was always small.

The old controversy over doctrine broke out again. George Whitefield was no longer present to project his spirit of reconciliation, but again both sides finally made adjustments, confessed their bad manners, and made their peace.

The excellent work Whitefield had nurtured in America was in trouble, too. John Wesley's problems were multiplying, but he faced them in the same straightforward manner for which he had long been famous. There were many thousands of Methodists in America by 1776, with no ordained men to administer the sacrament. And there were no Episcopal bishops willing to bestow orders on Methodist preachers. The touchy question that had nearly separated Charles and John a few years earlier was about to raise its head again.

John drew up a *Deed of Declaration* which legally defined "the conference of the people called Methodists," authorizing that body to appoint preachers after his and Charles's deaths. At the same time, he assumed the right to ordain.

In England it was an absurdity to think of a priest ordaining a bishop. John, unlike Charles, was a renegade in the eyes of most Anglicans in that he considered the orders of bishops and priests identical and apostolic succession a fable. To exercise that opinion in England was not practical. Chief Justice Mansfield, in answer to a question posed by Charles, made a singular judgment: "Ordination is separation."

In America, it was different. America had gained its independence with no national church. John didn't pretend to ordain bishops in the modern sense but according to his view of primitive episcopacy. Hence, in Methodism, the term *bishop* came to mean simply "chief pastor" or "general superintendent."

On the first day of September 1784, John Wesley laid hands on Dr. Thomas Coke, ordaining him superintendent of Methodism in America. Coke was an Oxford graduate and an ordained Anglican clergyman. Francis Asbury, although of little training, was a most effective preacher. He was likewise ordained bishop (by Bishop Coke) and did a monumental work in America.

Charles reluctantly concurred.

CHAPTER XVI

"The Best of All Is . . ."

By 1780, the Wesleys were growing old. John was seventy-seven; Charles, seventy-three. Both were in reasonably good health and had no thought of retiring. By then, John Wesley had ridden horseback or by light carriage more than 240,000 miles and preached no less than sixty thousand times. Charles and eight hundred full-time lay evangelists had not been idling.

During the decade of the 1780s, Methodism was about to become a denomination, disassociating itself from the mother church. John and Charles, however, remained Anglicans to their deaths. While they were determined to see a political and moral revolution—which alone could save the Commonwealth from national disaster such as France was facing—the Wesleys were basically revivalists. Putting first things first was their philosophy. They saw movements for the betterment of society underway, but the Wesleys realized that only a great spiritual awakening could provide a climate in which badly needed reforms might succeed in eighteenth-century England.

Britain had long indulged slavery. African bondsmen, numbering 14,000, were laboring on the estates of English gentlemen at the time the Wesleys and Whitefield were preaching to thousands of underpaid colliers in the mines near Bristol.

In the city of Durham, far to the north of London near Newcastle, lived an eccentric reformer named Granville Sharp. Sharp, a devout Quaker who was greatly inspired and motivated by the Methodist revival, began a crusade to free the slaves. He studied English law, satisfying himself that slavery was illegal in the British Isles. He took his case straight to the most eminent lawyers, including the mighty Sir William Blackstone. Forcing his way past an army of clerks, he refused to be daunted in his quest until he saw the problem laid on the desk of the crown's chief justice, William Mansfield. Whether Granville Sharp could have gained audience with this most prominent of jurists without the help of Charles Wesley is doubtful.

Chief Justice Mansfield had been the small boy at Westminster School whom Charles had once befriended, fighting off two bullies harassing the little fellow. Charles never forgot that young William thanked him, saying, "I'll repay you when I can. I promise." Mansfield never forgot it, either.

The justice took Granville's case for the bondsmen under careful consideration. The letter of the law was gospel to the jurist. Mansfield found that Granville Sharp had rightly interpreted the statutes. After a long, bitter fight in the courts, on June 22, 1772, 14,000 slaves in England gained their freedom.

By then, there was no stopping Granville Sharp. To put an end to the slave trade in which England was more deeply involved than any other nation on earth had long been his goal. By the time of the American revolution, England had supplied three million slaves to the English, French, and Spanish colonists. The man on the street in London was not aware of the evil involved. He was told that the slave trade was a type of missionary venture— evangelism of a kind, transporting millions of souls out of darkness to a land of light where Christ was preached, proper food was provided, and doctors were available when sickness and accident occurred. Even a crusader like Granville Sharp was only partially aware of the atrocities involved.

Granville was fully cognizant of the uphill battle he faced, for the slave trade was not only profitable business but also national policy. England's economy depended upon it. He was likewise aware that the Wesleyan revival was changing the attitude of the British Empire, making success in his dream at least a possibility.

An incident aboard the slave ship *Zong* brought the despicable problem into focus. Among the slaves on the *Zong,* headed for the West Indies, was a sharp, young black man who in Africa had come under the influence of a missionary through whom he gained a working knowledge of the English language. His African name being hard to pronounce, he was later given the nickname of Benji. Wisely, Benji kept his superior knowledge a secret, hoping to listen in on conversations that might assist him someday in making an escape.

During a severe tropical storm, Benji lay chained with his unfortunate companions in the filth and stench of their crowded quarters. Out on high seas, the ship was driven off course until it seemed hopelessly lost. After the storm, the captain was giving serious consideration to having 130 slaves thrown overboard to conserve food and water. Benji heard bits of conversation revealing the diabolic plan. Later, when some of the slaves were loosed on deck while others were cleaning the hold, Benji arranged with a friendly sailor to lower a rope to the water in case he (Benji) was among those cast away.

The drastic order was carried out in the darkness of night, drowning 129 innocent bondsmen. Benji clambered hand over hand up the rope and lost himself among the blacks aboard.

Later in a Puerto Rican port, he overheard several seamen talking about Granville Sharp.

"This Granville fellow ought to be horsewhipped," spat a drunken sea captain to his friends. "He figured somehow thet slavery wuz agin the law in England. He carried his notion clear up to the top and got ever' last one of them blacks set free. Now he's trying to throw the whole slave trade out the same window. Then where will we be?"

Benji vowed he would get to England someday and see this Granville Sharp. His opportunity came sooner than he expected, for his new owner took him to England as his valet.

Granville Sharp was greatly incensed by Benji's description of the atrocities common to the slave trade, which were ten times worse than he had suspected. The Quakers had condemned it in 1724. John Wesley had quarreled with Whitefield concerning it. But only a black man who had suffered the living death could picture it in all its horror.

Granville immediately prepared to file suit for murder against the company, naming the captain in particular. The underwriters who were being asked to reimburse the captain for his great loss were suing also. Again the case was laid at the feet of Lord Mansfield. No one knows for sure what the great jurist's real attitude in the matter may have been, but he had to judge according to the letter of the law. He had no choice.

"According to the statutes," he wrote, "it is exactly as if horses had been thrown overboard."

Granville Sharp understood that it was up to Parliament to change the law. An attempt to see this accomplished was his next course of action, but he needed a member of that august body to carry the fight. And just such a man had recently been elected to Parliament: William Wilberforce. Wilberforce was a small man of only twenty-one years—a gifted speaker with a brilliant mind and a natural crusading spirit. As a boy, he had been deeply influenced by the Methodists. Granville Sharp arrested the interest of the young statesman immediately.

"I will take the matter under serious consideration," Wilberforce promised him, "but don't expect a miracle over night. It will take a lot of men a lot of years—even with Providence on our side—to break through a wall as high and broad as this one."

The battle to outlaw the slave trade was a hard one indeed. Such a controversial issue had not been introduced in Parliament for at least a hundred years. A more experienced man than Wilberforce—even with his drive to right the monstrous wrong—would never attempt it. But Wilberforce was counting on a multitude of Methodists and a great host of friends both in and out of organized religious circles to pray for his success. Sensing his spiritual need, he was finally converted under the ministry of Whitefield and became a loyal friend of the Wesleys. His backing was even greater than he had hoped. Pressures were brought to bear through certain areas of the press and at the polls.

While the sons of Susanna didn't live to see the victory finally won, they gave the movement their full support to the very end.

How extensively American history was influenced by the eighteenth-century awakening can only be surmised. Certainly, the Declaration of Independence and the Constitution—from its preamble through the Bill of Rights and the amendments—reflect the Wesleyan spirit. Membership in American Methodist societies by 1776 numbered 3,148. Eight years later, the number had grown to 14,988. In 1791, it reached an amazing 42,000. The "new nation, conceived in liberty and dedicated to the proposition that all men are created equal," was literally rocked in the cradle of the great revival. While it took another eighty-five years to resolve the slavery question in the Western world, it was indeed finally accomplished.

The 1780s were not easy ones for Charles Wesley. He became a disappointed man, deeply concerned that none of his three children had accepted Christ. Why he could lead thousands of souls to the Lord, yet fail to convince his own young ones of their need of salvation was an unanswered question that bothered him incessantly.

Charles, Jr., was a bit eccentric and never strong. He made a living teaching music and playing occasionally in concerts, sometimes even before the royal family.

Daughter Sally was not musically inclined, but she

inherited her father's gift for composing verse. Neither she nor Charles, Jr., married.

Young Samuel developed into a composer and an organist of such unusual talent that he was sometimes called the father of modern English organ. He married and raised a family of musicians, one of whom was Samuel Sebastian Wesley, a highly esteemed composer in his own right. Among Sebastian's well-known compositions are "Blessed Be the God and Father," and "Thou Art My God."

Charles Wesley, his age showing plainly by 1787, failed to fully appreciate the genius of his progeny. Son Samuel became a trial to him because of an inability to live within his income. Then came another blow. Seeing a lucrative position open for an organist in a Catholic church, Samuel joined that body, nearly breaking his father's heart.

The mother took it all in stride, calmly praying every day for the promised "all things" of Romans 8:28, while caring for her family.

Charles wrote the nearly unbelievable total of 8,900 poems, the last of which he was still composing in his old age.

Two elements of joy and satisfaction were never lost to Charles and Sally through all their tribulations. One was a deep, abiding faith in God that they had shared for nearly forty years. The other, a love for one another that might well be the prime example for the marriages of all time.

Physically, John Wesley had never been as robust as his brother Charles. Through extended exposure to the elements as he pursued his exhausting schedule year after year, he seems to have developed a mild case of tuberculosis. He was convinced, however, that the rugged, out-of-door life kept him alive. He also suffered from hydrosis, a disease of the sweat glands that caused him a great deal of distress.

On one occasion, while laboring in North Ireland, John developed a high fever and took to his bed. He lost all his strength. His mind was affected, causing him to lose his memory. His friends were shocked to see his swollen tongue turn a sickly gray. For a time, they could find no pulse. Then suddenly it came to life, beating 130 times per minute.

Soon all hope for John's recovery was gone. In glaring headlines, the newspapers announced that the great evangelist was dead. Charles received the word with a further note that he must be prepared to stand in the gap. But all were wrong: the wiry, little preacher recovered and soon was back on his grueling schedule.

John, in his eighties, appeared stronger than he had been in a decade. Charles was ailing. John wrote to him, saying, "Dear brother, you must go out every day or die. Do not die to save charges. You certainly need not want anything as long as I live."

But alas! John's good advice did not avail. Charles's strength continued to desert him until he was forced to remain in bed. Then, early in April 1788, while John was preaching near Newcastle, a letter that had been misdirected was handed to him. He paused to open it, discovering that on March 29, his brother had gone to meet the Lord he had served so well. John, usually capable of controlling his emotions, bowed his head and burst into tears. The congregation wept with him.

Later, when he returned to London, Sally gave him the details of her husband's passing.

"Charles wasn't sick," she said. "He had no pain or fever. The wheel of the cistern didn't break—it just wore out."

No brother-in-law or uncle could have treated Sally and her family with greater liberality and tender care than did John Wesley. He sensed their problems and provided for every need. They loved him. And when the aged preacher would return to his home in London for a few days of badly needed rest, Sally and her daughter always saw that his house was in order and his every need fulfilled.

John suffered one regret over which he had no control. Charles, in his dying hours, asked that he not be buried by City Road Chapel where John had planned that their worn-out bodies should rest in peace together. Charles's Anglican heritage was too strong. At his request, his casket was carried by six ordained Episcopal rectors to the graveyard (consecrated ground) back of the old parish church of Maryelebone in London.

Riding in a carriage behind two spirited horses—a shawl around his shoulders and a rug across his knees—John Wesley, at the advanced age of eighty-four, continued to ride the old itinerant trail. All the persecution and harassment he faced in bygone days had melted away beneath the love and warmth of the gospel. Now, hardly a church was closed to him, but he preferred to preach in the open meadows with room for all who would hear the glorious truth of redemption. And nearly every priest and pastor attended his services, extending warm welcomes for his return.

Slowly but surely, the aging body tired. John began to

spend longer periods at home. Finally, his infrequent preaching missions were limited to the area around London, but his message never changed. The response to his appeals remained as great as ever. Among his final papers, these words were found: "It seemed that all who heard were, for the present, almost persuaded to be Christians."

John, standing with assistance beneath a white ash tree, preached his final field-sermon on October 6, 1790. He was in his eighty-seventh year. But John Wesley's ministry was not at an end. Without realizing it, he continued to preach "without ceasing" wherever he went. The people gazed upon the patriarch of Methodism with veneration, reaching for his trembling hand as he walked the streets, smiling his greeting. "Believe on the Lord Jesus Christ and thou shalt be saved," he repeated over and over again.

But John was not as senile as some of the people may have suspected. Alone in his room, he continued to keep up his diary and pen important letters to his preachers who missed his visits and advice. All his old talent of expression remained intact. And typically, he planned another journey to the north to be made in March 1791.

But during the winter, his strength failed. After preaching one last sermon at City Road Chapel in February, John Wesley took to his bed for the last time.

Even so, he kept abreast of the news. When he read of the difficulty William Wilberforce was facing in his fight to end the slave trade, he asked for pen and paper. His mind was remarkably clear but his hand unsteady. With great effort, John Wesley wrote the last letter of his life: a missive to encourage his young friend and crusader to keep up the fight, for surely God was on his side:

My dear sir,

Unless the Divine Power has raised you up to be as Athanasius, *contra mundum,* I see not how you can go through your glorious enterprise in opposing that execrable villainy which is the scandal of religion, of England, and of human nature. Unless God has raised you up for this very thing, you will be worn out by the opposition of men and devils; but *if God be for you, who can be against you?* Are all of them together stronger than God? Oh, *be not weary in well doing.* Go on, in the name of the Lord and in the power of His might, till even American slavery, the vilest that ever saw the sun, shall vanish away before it.

Reading a tract this morning written by a poor African, I was particularly struck by that circumstance that a man who has a black skin, being wronged or outraged by a white man, can have no redress; it being a law in our colonies that the oath of a black against a white goes for nothing. What villainy is this! That He who has guided you from your youth up, may continue to strengthen you in this and in all things, is the prayer of

> Your affectionate servant,
> John Wesley

John was so weary when he finished writing that he dropped the letter on the bed beside him. Then he drifted off to sleep. He awakened later when Sally entered his room, holding a paper in her hand.

"I have something to share with you that shall encourage your heart," she said.

John raised up and smiled as Sally straightened his

pillow. "Any bit of encouragement," he answered, "will be the best medicine I've had all day."

"Charles Junior and Sally are both seeking the Lord," she told him, fighting to contain her tears. "They are really in earnest. I'm sure they will find that 'peace that passeth all understanding' soon."

John was right. That was just the medicine he needed.

"Samuel is leaving the Catholic church," she continued. "He knows now that he joined it purely for the sake of expediency. He needed a job, you know."

"Yes," John answered. "I remember my brother was deeply disturbed when it happened. I tried to ease his concern. 'It's only a heart that is wrong,' I told him. 'Isn't every true believer ready for heaven?' I asked."

"I remember that," said Sally. "Charles Junior remembers it, too. That is helping him now in his seeking."

Two visitors appeared at the door. Sally stepped aside as they entered the room and conversed briefly with their ailing friend. When they left, John picked up the letter he had written to Wilberforce.

"I'm so weak, Sally, that I tire easily. I must rest, but before you go, I want to give you this letter for the post. I have written a thousand letters, but this one sapped my strength and took so long that I fear it shall be my last."

"Oh, that reminds me," Sally answered sadly. "I have here Charles's last poem. He was too weak to write, so he dictated it to me."

"Read it to me, please," cried John. "I wouldn't miss it for the world."

Sally read:

> *In age and feebleness extreme,*
> *Who shall a sinful worm redeem?*

> *Jesus, my only hope thou art,*
> *Strength of my failing flesh and heart;*
> *Oh, could I catch a smile from thee*
> *And drop into eternity.*

John, growing weaker by the hour, lived on for several days. Sally and her daughter, along with several close friends, were in the room March 2, 1791, as the end was drawing near. John raised his hand and tried to speak. His only audible word was a faint "Farewell."

The last of the *sons of Susanna* was going home. But the man about whom more books would be written than of any religious leader since the apostle Paul had yet one message to deliver. He visibly inhaled as he tried to raise his head. Then, with the last half-ounce of strength remaining, he spoke in the resonant tone of earlier days, *"The best of all is, God is with us!"*

Epilogue

The last of the sons of Susanna remained on the field of action until one of the greatest spiritual awakenings of the centuries had penetrated every community, rich and poor, of Britain. It had likewise invaded the continent and in America had reached westward into and beyond every frontier.

The revival continued to roll for years to come. Its salutary effect upon theological liberals of the era as well evangelicals of other persuasions can hardly be exaggerated.

Beyond the spiritual uplift of the revival, its influence for good upon the moral and political climate of the times has long been a matter of record.

Harold Nicolson, in *The Age of Reason,* sums up: "Lecky goes so far as to state that it was Methodism which at the end of the eighteenth century preserved England from a revolution as terrible as that of France. . . . It passed on to the evangelicals its high ideals of public duty; by its example it reformed and raised the Church of England; it purified politics, gave a fresh stimulus to public education, and created the wave of humanitarianism that led to the abolition of slavery and [to] penal reform."*

---

* Quoted by Garth Lean in *Strangely Warmed* (Wheaton, Ill.: Tyndale House Publishers, 1982), 126-127.